Today was the day she intended to confront Lucky Welch.

Suddenly, Lucky was heading straight for her with a lanky walk that screamed pure cowboy. His belt buckle was even bigger than his confident stride. He wiped dust from his hat, smiled, and Natalie thought maybe he had the whitest teeth she'd ever seen. Another bull rider walked beside him.

Natalie stopped in her tracks. Lucky stopped, too, and caught her eye. "Do you want an autograph?"

Oh, no! He thought she was a buckle bunny. In a way, his assumption knocked down the defenses she'd so carefully erected while she was watching him.

"No," she blurted, "I don't want an autograph. I want help with Marcus's son."

Books by Pamela Tracy

Love Inspired

Daddy for Keeps

Love Inspired Suspense

Pursuit of Justice
Broken Lullaby

PAMELA TRACY

lives in Arizona with a newly acquired husband (*Yes, Pamela is somewhat a newlywed. You can be a newlywed for seven years. We're only on year five*) and a confused cat (*Hey, I had her all to myself for fifteen years. Where'd this guy come from? But, maybe it's okay. He's pretty good about feeding me and petting me*) and a toddler (*Newlymom is almost as fun as newlywed!*). She was raised in Omaha, Nebraska, and started writing at age twelve (*A very bad teen romance featuring David Cassidy from the Partridge Family*). Later, she honed her writing skills while earning a BA in Journalism at Texas Tech University in Lubbock, Texas (*And wrote a very bad science fiction novel that didn't feature David Cassidy*).

Readers can write to her at www.pamelakayetracy.com, or c/o Steeple Hill Books, 233 Broadway, Suite 1001, New York, NY 10279.

Daddy for Keeps
Pamela Tracy

Steeple
Hill®

Published by Steeple Hill Books™

STEEPLE HILL BOOKS

Steeple
Hill®

Recycling programs
for this product may
not exist in your area.

ISBN-13: 978-0-373-87514-6
ISBN-10:   0-373-87514-2

DADDY FOR KEEPS

Copyright © 2009 by Pamela Tracy Osback

Printed in U.S.A.

Every good and perfect gift is from above, coming down from the Father of the heavenly lights, who does not change like shifting shadows.

— *James* 1:17

To every mother who gave her heart at first sight, first touch, first cry.

Plus, special thanks to Mark Henley, who shared bull riding expertise. The ride in the last chapter is really his. And to Wendy Lemme, who read the book in its final stage and helped with fine-tuning.

Chapter One

The billboard on top of the grocery store featured a picture they'd taken straight from his mother's photo album. Lucky Welch, headliner of this year's Selena Rodeo, shook his head and hoped no one recognized the bull in the background. It had belonged to his grandfather and was a family pet named Whimper.

Pulling out his cell, Lucky punched in his mother's number. She didn't even bother with "hello." Instead, in a no-nonsense voice, she said, "Lucky, I'm right here with Bernice. She says it's silly to pay good money to stay at a campground when you're surrounded by family."

Surrounded by family was a bit of a stretch, but Lucky knew better than to mention that detail. "Mom—" He paused, knowing that no matter what he said, he'd be staying at Bernice's. That Bernice Baker was his mother's best friend from childhood and not really family had never been an argument that worked. Nope, his mother always had one better, like…

"Bernice has already changed the sheets in Mary's room."

The changing of the sheets for company, at least in his

family and most West Texas families, for that matter, was a
time-honored tradition and not one to mess with. Plus, Lucky
had met bulls easier to win over than his mother. Well, okay,
one bull, to be exact: Whimper.

An hour later he pulled his truck into Bernice's yard and
waited for the fireworks. They came in the shape of his mother
and her best friend, who exploded out the front door and
down to meet him.

Since his brother's death six months ago, his mother had
taken excitable to a new level. After assuring her he was
doing just fine—well, fine for a bull rider who'd put 52,000
miles on his truck this year—he unpacked in Bernice's oldest
daughter's bedroom. He stuffed his rigging bag into a closet
already full of old clothes, old shoes and old suitcases. He
piled his Blackwood spurs and hand-tooled leather chaps on
top of a hope chest that Mary had often referred to as
hope*less*. Slightly older and full of jokes and mischief, Mary
had taught him that girls could be tough but that sometimes
the toughness was an act.

His mother and Bernice waited for him on the porch,
enjoying the sunset. Polar opposites, they'd been friends since
their first day of high school. Lucky's mother, Betsy Welch,
had ridden the bus an hour each way from a neighboring
town. She stood almost six feet tall and still favored the big
hair of her generation. Bernice had always called Selena,
Texas, home. She edged just over the five-foot mark and was
nearly as round as she was tall. She still wore her hair tied
back in a simple ponytail. She'd been the tomboy; Lucky's
mother had been the princess and Selena's rodeo queen when
she was just eighteen.

"We're going to have fried chicken later on," Bernice said.

"Sounds good, but I want to check out the town."

"You mean the competition," his mother guessed.

"Yup."

Lucky headed for his truck. Bernice's young son, Howard Junior, called Howie by everyone, followed Lucky down the path. "I'm gonna be a bull rider when I grow up," he bragged.

Ten-year-old Howie looked like he should still be pushing cars on the ground, watching cartoons or carrying a snake and chasing girls—not planning to hop on the backs of bulls. "You practice every day?" Lucky asked.

"Nope."

"Then you're not gonna be a bull rider."

"Yes, I am," Howie insisted stubbornly.

"You gonna practice every day?"

"Don't haf to."

Lucky grinned and ruffled Howie's hair. "Okay, if you say so." Howie scowled in return, as Lucky put the truck in gear and headed to a town temporarily doubled in size because of the rodeo *he* headlined. The town was one long street of businesses flanked by modest homes. Tonight, the bowling alley had a full parking lot, the restaurants had long lines and music blared from a bar on the corner of Fifth Avenue and Main.

Man, he wanted to take the highway to the Lubbock rodeo. His buddies were all there, and the purse was way bigger. When they heard he was doing Selena, they'd either laughed or offered condolences. He couldn't decide which was more fitting. Most claimed his absence from the Lubbock rodeo was the answer to their prayers.

They had less competition, and he had a very happy mother.

Her roots were in the Selena area and although now she was a big-city girl, he knew deep in her heart she'd rather be here. If this rodeo made her happy, fine, he'd do it.

He found a parking spot at the end of the street, walked to a hamburger joint and stood in a ridiculously long line. He watched teenagers talking on their cell phones instead of to each other. Husbands his age divided their time between watching their children climb on the indoor jungle gym and talking with their wives.

Life.

That's what he was witnessing. Ordinary, daily life. People who were doing the most routine activities: talking, eating, playing, sharing. Not at all like his own solitary life. Lucky shook his head to clear his thoughts. Man, he needed to shake this melancholy mood. Since Marcus's death, dark moods and the desire to be alone kept popping up at the most inopportune times. His gloom had already cost him too much money and too much time. Tonight, the need to get away and brood had cost him homemade fried chicken.

He finally snagged a meal and headed for a seat. Bowing his head, Lucky spoke to his Heavenly Father, asking for forgiveness, healing and help.

When he lifted his head, not only were the fries cold but also his appetite. Maybe it took a bit more than six months and a thousand prayers to get over the loss of a brother, a brother who'd loved Bernice's fried chicken, a brother who had also loved the rodeo life.

Yup, this part of Texas brought back all kinds of emotions. When Marcus and Lucky were young, they'd left the overcrowded streets of Austin and spent memorable summers with their grandparents in a town even smaller than this one, just forty-five miles west of here. They'd even come here for the Selena Rodeo, not only because his mother loved her memory of being a rodeo queen but also because during his younger days Grandpa had been a bull rider. He'd ridden in the first Selena Rodeo. He'd started the passion. And he'd emphasized the danger.

Lucky paid attention; Marcus didn't.

Now Lucky had spent the last six months trying to forgive his only brother for dying.

Dying before he found his way back home.

Six months ago and on his fifth ride of the day, Marcus made his eight seconds, jumped from the bull and was knocked unconscious by a quick turn of the bull's head. Then, before the clowns could intervene, Marcus was stepped on, butted, trampled and broken in front of hundreds. And Lucky had seen it all, hopeless to stop the tragedy.

A friend had kept Lucky from climbing the fence and running to his brother while the bull still raged.

Marcus died.

In a matter of seconds.

He died.

Lucky unwrapped the hamburger he didn't really want and took a bite that had no flavor. A toddler stumbled by with a French fry clutched in one hand and a tennis shoe in the other. He hit the ground, bounced back up, grabbed the French fry from the floor, shoved it in his mouth and moved on. One of the women laughed, and suddenly, Lucky noticed just how beautiful she really was. How alive. Even as she cleaned the face of a high-chair-bound baby, she touched her husband's hand.

"*...But the woman is the glory of man.*" Lucky unwittingly recalled the familiar Bible verse. Lucky had not experienced the glory of a wife to call his own, but Marcus had married once.

It lasted five months, probably because Marcus was seldom around. After that, his brother had spent the next three years in and out of relationships. Most had lasted weeks, one quite a bit longer, but never with women who could be considered the "forever" type.

Lucky shook his head. His thoughts didn't bode well for

tomorrow's rodeo. Thinking about his brother hadn't made the last six months easier, hadn't helped his standings on the circuit, hadn't put money in his pocket. Good thing the previous three years had. He had almost quit after Marcus died. Truthfully, Lucky stayed in only because of the memories. That and the Sunday morning worship that gave Lucky hope that maybe he'd help some other Marcus find his way home.

Lucky threw the remains of his meal in the trash can and headed outside. The dark Texas sky greeted him. He didn't want to go back to Bernice's or head for the bar to see who he knew, *who he could drive home.* He leaned against the restaurant wall and looked down Main Street. There were at least four bars, two restaurants, a bank and a church.

Lucky wished there were four churches, two restaurants, a bank and an empty bar with a For Sale sign in its window. Some of the circuit riders called Lucky a preacher because he carried a Bible, could quote scriptures without hesitation, and, yes, frequented the bars when the rodeo came to town.

Not to drink. Nope, he'd put down the bottle the first time a drunk Marcus was hauled to jail after wrapping his truck around a tree. Lucky had come to despise the bottle after watching Marcus pour his money, talent and friends down the drain while under its influence. Now Lucky frequented bars in order to drive his friends to their motels, their trailers and, yes, even to the homes of the girls who followed the rodeo, "buckle bunnies," who were so lost Lucky didn't know what scripture to begin with. Lucky crossed the parking lot, climbed into his truck and pointed it down the familiar street.

Tears—hot, instant and completely unwelcome—blurred yet another oversize image of Lucky Welch. Natalie Crosby almost turned on the windshield wipers, but windshield wipers only worked when it was raining outside the vehicle, not when the wetness came from her own eyes.

Gripping the steering wheel of her aged Chevrolet, she managed to avoid running into the rodeo fans clustered at the gate. The poster beckoned rodeo fans to come to the fairgrounds, have fun and cheer on their favorite riders. What Natalie needed—wanted—was a giant dart and an even bigger target. Since that wasn't an option, it looked like a little emotional overload would have to do. Sensibly, she pulled into a parking spot a little farther from the entrance than she liked. It was either that or plow into a horse trailer.

"Mommy?" Robby wiggled in the backseat. He could see the activity outside and didn't want to be confined. Add to that Natalie's strange behavior, and no wonder she had a fidgety, confused little boy.

"I'm okay, Robby. Sit back." Natalie wiped at the tears and succeeded only in spreading the evidence of her despair instead of removing it.

After taking several deep breaths, she looked at the poster again and reminded herself there was no need for virtual darts. The man wasn't Marcus. Couldn't be. No way would Marcus be headlining Selena's premiere event of the year. He'd drawn the death bull six months ago, and his rodeo career ended with a ride in a hearse instead of a ride in a parade.

This rodeo rider was Marcus's little brother, Lucky. Some called him the Preacher. She'd never met him, but if she'd heard correctly, he was the antithesis of Marcus. He preached instead of partied and carried a Bible instead of a little black book.

Her cousin Tisha, who shared Natalie's last name, had little to say about Lucky, except that he didn't seem to like her much. Right now, the image of Lucky faced the crowd with an oversize, mirthful grin and impossible dark brown eyes that demanded notice.

Natalie checked the tiny rearview mirror she'd attached to her windshield. It allowed her to check on Robby while driving. She intended to make sure he had everything he needed, especially a good and stable home. Robby was responsible for her attendance today—Robby and this overgrown bull rider. Natalie hadn't graced the Selena rodeo in a decade and definitely didn't want to be here today.

"Mommy, why we sit still?" Robby battled with the buckle on his car seat. He was growing up way too fast, wanting to do things for himself. Still, she'd rather he battle the seat belt than notice the battle taking place in front of him.

Natalie gritted her teeth. No way could she explain her fears, her conflicts, to a three-year-old.

Someone thumped on the back fender of her car. Walter Hughes, her dad's best friend, waved as he hurried by. "We need to talk later," he mouthed. She was grateful he didn't stop. Questions would only make her rethink what she had to do, and Walter had known her since she was born. No way would he accept that she had stopped by the rodeo "just for the view."

For the last two weeks, since her father's death, Walter had called every evening to ask if she was all right.

Am I all right? Are we all right?

He probably knew that although she kept saying yes, the true answer was no. There was a huge hole in her world, one that tapped her on the shoulder every few minutes and whispered, *Wrong, everything feels wrong, something's missing.* She'd buried her father—made the phone calls, called in the obituary, filled out the forms, arranged the funeral, said all the right things—and today, she still felt wrong.

Walter was just as sad as she was. He'd gone to school with her father, been the best man at his wedding and, since retirement, they met almost every morning for breakfast at the café in town.

The hole that Natalie felt was no stranger to Walt. Plus, Walt felt a sense of responsibility for her. His family owned Selena's only bank. Although Walt no longer put in an eight-hour day, really not even an eight-minute day, he knew her situation—about the low checking account balance, about the surprise loan her dad had taken out just five months ago, using his business as collateral. Today, the business belonged to her dad's partner, who was as mystified by the sudden turn of events as she was. Natalie was left with nothing. It was Walt, one hundred percent, who did not believe her dad had left her in financial trouble.

Natalie wondered at the conviction of the banker. Surely as a banker, he knew that most Americans were one paycheck away from being homeless. Walt simply said that Leonard Crosby was not "most" Americans. He'd take care of his own. Walt wanted to look at the will, wanted to help, wanted to believe in something that just wasn't there.

Natalie could only think about what was there. She had a son and a home to take care of. Her part-time job as a Web designer allowed her to support herself and be a stay-at-home mom while her father was alive. But it wasn't a career that could support the large home that had been in her family for more than a hundred years. It was not a career that could pay for a college education for Robby. At least not on the hours she worked. She could do—would do—more. But to keep her family home she needed money now.

Worry, combined with overwhelming loss, was keeping her awake at night, staring out windows and trying to figure out a way to make a go of her—their—life.

And the billboard and posters all over town announcing the headliner of the Selena rodeo offered a dangerous solution that just contributed to her sorrow and angst.

It made her reconsider options she shouldn't be thinking about. It got her out of bed this morning as the clock radio glowed a bright orange six o'clock. It had her standing in front of her closet remembering what it felt like to dress as a participant. She'd almost cried at the combination of longing and fear that enveloped her.

Natalie pushed open the car door and stuck one leg out. And froze.

Why'd they have to put the poster at the only entrance?

Lucky was well-known for his participation in Cowboy Church, right? Surely that should count for something—some sort of commitment to responsibility. Natalie hadn't been to church since childhood, but she remembered some of the lessons. Jesus told His flock to take care of the widows and orphans, right?

Natalie wiped the last tears form her cheeks as Robby's "Mom! Mom! Mom!" caught her attention. She finally stepped out of the car carefully and went around to get her rodeo-clad son. Yup, Pop Pop, Robby's grandfather, had spent plenty of money creating a miniature cowboy, and this morning Natalie allowed Robby to dress the part. He wore a belt with his name, tiny boots, and even a pair of chaps. The only request that went unfulfilled from her son's Christmas wish list was a horse.

Pop Pop was willing; Natalie was not.

"Can I ride on a horse today?" Robby skidded down Natalie's leg and hit the ground. Natalie bit back both a yelp of pain and a too-abrupt comment. Robby wasn't old enough to understand her limp or her fears, and she didn't want to transfer her negative feelings about horses to him. Truth was, going to the rodeo had her in a sweat, and she didn't know what to blame for her troubles more: the rodeo or the rodeo cowboy.

"You can't ride a horse today, but there will be plenty of other things to do."

He glared at her, an accusing look on his face. Fun, she was denying him fun. Well, today wasn't about fun. It was about survival because today was the day she intended to confront Lucky Welch.

Salvation or ruination.

And what should she tell Robby? One thing for sure, she couldn't just lie down and die, or give up. She took Robby by the hand and led him to the poster. It was past time to take action, and Robby was three and could understand more than she gave him credit for. "This man…"

His face brightened, and he tried to help. "A cowboy?"

For a brief moment, Natalie considered pointing out the thick brown hair, dark brown eyes and strong chin so unlike her own blond, blue-eyed, elfin look.

And so like Robby's own thick dark hair, brown eyes and still-forming strong chin.

"Yes. I think I might know him."

"Really?" For the first time in days, Robby's eyes brightened. "A cowboy! You know a real cowboy? Can I meet him, Mommy?"

She opened her mouth to answer, but the words didn't come. She couldn't do this. Not right now. Not when her father had just died. Not when she was in danger of losing her home. But the loss of her father, the danger of losing her home, were exactly why she was standing here today, contemplating making the worst mistake of her life.

Because it might not be a mistake, it might be salvation.

The high school band warmed up in the distance. Two children eating cotton candy walked by. Natalie took a breath and managed a smile as nostalgia took her back to the days when the rodeo was a good place to be. *She and her dad, on*

rodeo day. Cotton candy sticking to her fingers. And the rodeo
still smelled the same, a mixture of popcorn, sweat—both
human and animal—and excitement. Yes, excitement had a
scent. Natalie first noted the aroma at the age of eight. She'd
been leading her pony, Patches, in the children's parade. To
think she'd worried the rodeo might have changed.

Well, everything else had.

Excitement attached itself to this rodeo, always had, and
it buzzed with an energy that even Robby picked up on. If she
hadn't put her hand on his shoulder, he'd have been all the
way to the ticket gate before she got her bearings. "There's
no rush. The day is just beginning."

He bobbed his head, clearly wishing he had free rein. *No
way, not here, not today.*

She turned, taking a step toward the entrance.

"Natalie, it's been forever since I've seen you at one of our
rodeos. You need any help?"

"No, thanks, I'm fine." Natalie nodded and forced herself
not to rub her thigh. "Good to see you, Allison." They'd been
fast friends during school, practiced together and competed
against each other in local barrel races events. Allison Needham, like Natalie's cousin Tisha, had gone on to be a rodeo
queen; Natalie reigned as a couch potato. Allison came back
from the road about three years ago, a quieter girl with a baby
on the way, and she didn't talk much about the past. She
didn't talk much to Natalie, either.

Natalie figured she had her cousin Tisha to thank for that.

"Good to see you, too. Travis is competing for the first
time. He'll be tickled to know you got to see it."

She and Allison had pushed her baby brother, Travis, in his
stroller, and now he was all grown up.

"I'll watch," Natalie promised.

Robby waited at the ticket booth. Natalie plunked down

her money and pushed through the gate. T-shirts were to her right, Native American art to her left. Robby headed straight to the food and smiled. "Hot dog?"

"We just ate breakfast."

"But I still hungry, Mommy."

"Nothing tastes better than a rodeo hot dog, Natalie." The comment came from one of her dad's friends, manning the concession booth. "My treat."

Natalie swallowed. This was harder than she'd thought possible. Why had she imagined that she could attend this rodeo and just melt into the crowd? She'd lived in Selena all her life, and she knew this was a time-honored event. Everyone would be here—from her old kindergarten teacher to the bank teller who handled the Crosby transactions.

"I appreciate the offer, but I'll pay." She added a soda for herself and held Robby's hand as they followed the crowd. He stopped to gape at the cowboys sitting on the fence.

Lucky Welch wasn't one of them.

The bleachers were already pretty full, and Robby frowned at the people who'd beaten him to the most coveted seats. "Mommy, we sit there." He pointed to a spot near the top. People were pressed together, and the walkway was crowded with spectators.

"Over here!" Patty Dunbar, her best friend, waved from the crowded bottom row. Robby headed right over and plopped down in Patty's lap.

"Oomph, I think you've gained a ton since the last time I saw you." Patty settled Robby next to her own son, Daniel, and scooted to make room for Natalie. "I cannot believe you're here."

"Me, neither. Where's the baby?"

"With my mother, and don't change the subject. Why are you here?" Patty whispered the question so only Natalie could hear. Ten years ago, Natalie broke her hip at this very rodeo. That had been enough reason to keep Natalie away. But, of course, that wasn't why Patty was asking.

Natalie knew exactly what Patty was really asking because Patty was the only one in Selena, besides Natalie, who knew who Robby's father was.

Before Natalie could respond, the "Star-Spangled Banner" boomed from the sound system and the grand entry began. Everyone stood, and the cowboys took off their hats. Natalie saw him then, in the arena, standing amidst a straight line of competitors with his hand over his heart. He was more compact than she'd imagined and looked more serious than some of his peers. He actually looked like he believed in, enjoyed, the national anthem.

Natalie spent the next few hours watching the steer wrestling and the team roping. She took Robby to the bathroom twice and then for a walk during the barrel racing, denying it was planned timing, not that Patty believed her, and the whole while Natalie pretended not to look for Lucky. Bareback bronc and saddle bronc riding were next; Robby was mesmerized. After that, she watched her son attempt to catch a greased pig and pretended not to look for Lucky again. This, of course, was followed by another trip to the bathroom.

Finally, it was time for the evening's final event—bull riding.

The term "crowd favorite" took on new meaning when Lucky Welch's turn came. He rode often, and he rode hard, scoring in the eighties on a bull named Corkscrew. To Natalie's eye, Lucky looked like a rag doll with one hand tied to a moving locomotive. She felt faint. What if he was killed? It only took one fall, one wrong move! She knew that from experience. So did Lucky. Just down the bleacher, a woman yelled, "You can do it, son!"

Leaning forward, all Natalie could see was big hair. Lucky's mother had been introduced to the crowd a few hours ago. Standing alongside Allison and other past queens, those who'd bothered to show up, Betsy Welch smiled, but the smile didn't quite reach her eyes.

Yes, the Welches would still be grieving Marcus the way Natalie and Robby were grieving her dad. Difference was, as Walt kept pointing out, Pop Pop took care of his own. Or at least tried to.

Marcus had only taken care of Marcus.

Next to Lucky's mother sat Bernice Baker. For the last year, really since Robby stopped looking like a baby and started looking like a Welch, every time Natalie saw the woman, she headed the opposite way.

Bernice Baker was probably the only person in town who might notice how much Robby looked like a Welch.

Long shot, but a shot nevertheless.

Natalie almost chuckled. Since Robby was a baby, she'd been worrying about Bernice, about Marcus showing up. Now she was willingly looking for Lucky Welch and thinking about confronting him. She was even worrying about the match between him and the bull.

The woman yelling "son" was only a basketball toss away, and Robby had no idea she was his paternal grandmother. Oh, no, no. This was not something Natalie could do after all. She changed her mind, started to stand, but she chose the wrong moment. She was stuck. She couldn't pull Robby left or right. Not while the crowd was this worked up, not at the climax of the rodeo. She stretched her leg, trying to ease the stiffness, and watched as Lucky Welch made the eight seconds and jumped from the bull to land on both feet. The bull made a move, Lucky ducked behind a clown, and it was over. The crowd roared. The scores to be announced, but finally the day's events ended. A human surge began exiting the rodeo. Robby, who'd never been to a rodeo, finally felt overwhelmed by the crowd and clutched at Natalie's hand. Daniel, a rodeo veteran at just five, headed for the edge of the arena. Patty was right behind.

Natalie panicked. If she saw Lucky, and he was alone, she'd approach him, she really would, but if she—

Suddenly, Lucky was heading straight for her with a swagger that screamed pure cowboy. His belt buckle was even bigger than his confident strides. He wiped dust from his hat, smiled, and Natalie thought maybe he had the whitest teeth she'd ever seen. Another bull rider walked beside him.

Natalie stopped in her tracks. Lucky stopped, too, and caught her eye. "Do you want an autograph?"

Oh, no! He thought she was a buckle bunny.

In a way, his assumption knocked down the defenses she'd so carefully erected while she was watching him. Unfortunately, she forgot to consider that the other side might not have a safety net. "No," she blurted, "I don't want an autograph. I want help with Marcus's son."

Chapter Two

Lucky had spent a lifetime learning how to harness control, and he wouldn't lose it now. Even if a buckle bunny was trying to tarnish his brother's memory.

The cowboy next to him looked at Lucky with a relieved expression, said, "I think this one's for you," and took off for the cowboy ready room.

The threat of paternity suits was a real issue to the boys on the circuit. Most played hard and all too often got mixed up with women who wanted bragging rights and/or a piece of the purse. Well, this gal had really missed the boat. What kind of woman showed up six months after a bull rider's death and…?

Lucky backed up. The noise of the crowd had boomed only a moment before, but now he didn't hear a thing. He could only look at the woman and the little boy by her side. She looked right back at him, young, curvy, blond, her eyes wide with fear. To his dismay, something registered, a glimpse of a memory.

No, it couldn't be.

"Tisha?" It had been over three years since he'd last seen

her. She looked different, but then hard living had a way of changing people.

It had certainly changed Marcus.

The woman's eyes narrowed. Tears disappeared, replaced by anger.

Marcus had dated Tisha Crosby for just over a year. She'd wiped out his bank account and his heart. Marcus hadn't been the same afterward. Maybe this was why. Lucky didn't know that much about kids, but the boy could be the right age. Plus, he had the look—the Welch look. Thick, dark brown hair, piercing brown eyes and the square chin that made shaving a time-consuming venture. Something akin to fear settled in Lucky's stomach.

Looked like the family roller coaster was about to switch into high gear again—thanks to Marcus.

The woman—it must be Tisha—clutched at the boy and pulled him close. Regret washed over her face, replacing the anger. Well, at least she cared for the boy. From what Lucky remembered, she'd been a cold, calculating woman. Not everyone saw past the beautiful facade she presented. Marcus hadn't.

"Never mind," she whispered. "We were wrong, so wrong, to come here. Come on, Robby, let's get out of here." She stumbled between two people. Robby—eyes wide—tried to hurry and keep up with her.

"Wait!" Lucky was at her side in two seconds.

"Leave us alone. It was my mistake." She held up a hand, stopping him, and somewhat regaining her composure. "We want nothing to do with you."

He started to follow her, and he would have, if he hadn't seen the tears streaming from the boy's eyes.

Lucky didn't want the boy—his nephew maybe?—to be afraid of him.

"Everything all right?" Three men, strong farmer types, materialized in front of him, blocking him. Their words were directed at the woman; their granite gazes were aimed at him. Lucky stopped. As for Tisha, she wasn't taking the time to answer. Just like that, he lost track of Marcus's son. The woman had him by the hand and was hurrying him through the crowd.

"I just need to talk to her," Lucky said. He took one step then halted as the men angled for a block. They looked meaner than the bull he'd just ridden.

"It looks like she doesn't want to talk to you," the biggest one said.

"Tisha!" he hollered. He took a step and then noted that, if anything, the three men had moved closer. He considered his options. Three against one was more than he bargained for, especially when some blond-haired woman, her purse all primed to bash him upside the head, joined the fray.

"Tisha," the blonde spat. "You think she's Tisha?"

"Isn't she?" Lucky croaked.

"No, that's Natalie. She happens to be Tisha's cousin, but that's all the resemblance there is."

He saw the woman then, leaving the front gate, with the little boy. He could see now that her uneven gait wasn't fatigue, the earlier stumble was not clumsiness. She stopped by a small car parked in a handicapped spot. Yup, the limp was real.

He'd have to rethink this encounter, which might have been his all-time low.

The next time he said a prayer, he'd have so much to say it might take him a year to get to "Amen." Especially since he had no intention of sharing this information with his family until he was sure. It wasn't the first time Marcus had been accused of fatherhood. But this time, the child looked like a Welch, and somehow Tisha was involved.

He nodded at the three men before they could move any closer, skipped the ready room and, still in his gear, headed for his truck. Intuition told him Robby was indeed Marcus's son. More than intuition told him his mother would never understand Lucky not sharing the discovery with her immediately. In essence, he was robbing her of precious days of grandmotherhood.

But gut feelings were not always reliable. Otherwise, Lucky would hold a few more titles and have a lot more money and a whole lot fewer broken bones. He'd look into this Natalie woman and wait before telling his mother, even though keeping the secret might be a crime he'd pay for later.

Once Lucky had opened the truck's door and climbed behind the wheel, he dialed his lawyer—not that he expected the man could be reached on a Saturday night. After letting the phone ring until it went to voice mail, Lucky left a quick message for him to call, hung up and stared out the truck's windows. Without exception, the festive mood of the rodeo carried over to the dirt parking lot. Exhausted-looking children clutched treats, toys and their parents' hands. Adults laughed, took sips of soda and reached for the ones they loved.

Normal, so normal.

Once again, Lucky's emotional roller coaster crested a steep incline.

"Every good and perfect gift is from above, coming down from the Father of the heavenly lights, who does not change like shifting shadows."

The Bible verse came suddenly and comforted his spirit. He pocketed his phone, shed his gear and headed into town. There was a dance, there were bars, there were plenty of places to go to find out what he most wanted to know. Based on how quickly the farmer types had circled, Lucky figured

Natalie was well-known and well-liked in Selena. Before he met up with her again, he wanted a little history, some semblance of equal footing.

On her *and her cousin Tisha*.

He drove down the middle of town, intent on stopping somewhere but seeing no place where he'd feel comfortable. The tent on the fairgrounds holding tonight's dance was too crowded and upbeat, the bars in town too crowded and dark. He turned around and cruised again. Finally, he settled on a 1950s-style diner on the edge of town with plenty of horse trailers in the parking lot. Surely he'd run into not only peers but also locals inside. As long as the three farmer types were content to stab chicken-fried steaks instead of him, he'd be good.

He didn't even make it inside the door.

"Lucky Welch. Wow, I enjoyed watching you! Where you going next?"

The man was a young local and today had been his first competition. Travis Needham, Lucky remembered. He had spunk but was as clumsy as a puppy. He hadn't known how to handle his draw, scored dead last and had enjoyed every minute of the rodeo. Lucky envied him. The first few years he and Marcus rodeoed had been magic.

"Not sure," Lucky said as he looked around. There were plenty of familiar faces, but most were seated at tables with no empty spaces.

"Join us," Travis invited. *Us* looked to be a young woman and older man, both looking a lot like Travis.

Never look a gift horse in the mouth. His grandfather had actually been talking about horses when he shared the proverb, but today Lucky knew it had more than one meaning. "Thanks." He sat next to Travis and directly across from the older man. Putting out his hand, he said, "I'm Luc—"

"I know who you are, son." The man put down his fork and returned the handshake. "Travis has been talking about you for months, ever since you accepted the invitation to headline the rodeo. I'm Fred Needham. Guess you can tell by looking, these two belong to me. Sure enjoyed seeing a pro today."

"Selena holds a nice rodeo."

"I've seen you compete quite a few times." Travis's sister didn't hold out her hand although she'd set her fork aside the moment he sat down. If anything, she looked a bit reticent.

"Allison, don't bring it up," Travis urged.

"Bring what up?" Lucky asked.

"I was at the rodeo, the Denton rodeo," she whispered. "I'm sorry, so sorry."

Denton…six months ago, where everything went wrong.

"Yeah, I'm sorry, too." He looked at Allison. She looked right back at him, and he got the feeling that if it had been up to her, he would not have been invited to join them. He didn't know why. He'd never seen her before. "Did you know Marcus?"

"I knew him because of Tisha."

Fred frowned. Lucky waited a moment, trying to figure out if the frown came because of Marcus or Tisha. If he were a father, he'd keep his daughters away from men like Marcus and his sons away from women like Tisha.

Finally, Travis filled in the silence. "Allison and Tisha were roommates for a while. Allison used to rodeo. She was in Denton cheering on a friend."

Allison nodded. "I used to rodeo. When I practice, I can do the cloverleaf in eighteen seconds without touching a single barrel. When it's the real thing, the barrels move in front of me."

Travis nodded. "I've seen them sprout legs. Ain't pretty. Now, the way you ride that bull is magic, Lucky. I didn't realize your mama had been a one-time rodeo queen here in Selena."

"I told him," Fred said. "He just didn't listen."

A harried waitress found their table, refilled the Needhams' iced teas, cleared plates and took Lucky's order.

Travis took a long drink and then said, "Man, it was a treat to have you competing. This turned out to be the biggest rodeo Selena ever hosted. We had cowboys show up today who always bypass us in favor of Lubbock."

Lucky smiled. "I had fun."

"Where'd you learn to sit the bull? My dad's always helped me, plus all the guys around here do bull outs on Saturday night."

"You know where Delaney is?"

Fred nodded. "It's about forty-five miles west of here. Not much there."

"My grandparents lived there. Grandpa actually competed against the legend Jim Shoulders. I don't think Grandpa ever won a thing, but man, he loved the bulls. He taught my brother and me what equipment to buy, which hand to favor, how to get off and how to get away."

"How old were you?" Allison asked.

"He started us when we were ten, but it was mostly play. Then, when we hit thirteen, he took us as far as we'd let him."

"Only forty-five miles from here." Travis shook his head. "I had no idea you were so close."

"It's a small world," Lucky agreed. "My mom even went to high school here in Selena."

There wouldn't be a better opportunity, so he looked at Allison and said, "So, you traveled with Tisha. Did you know my brother?"

Allison paled. "Tisha was just beginning to date him when I was bunking with her. Pretty soon I didn't bunk with her anymore. I went on my own—"

"Came back home," Fred interrupted.

"—soon after they started getting serious."

"I tried to warn you about that girl," Fred said.

Allison's lips pressed together in a look of agitation Lucky knew all too well. "Dad," she said. "Leave it be."

"Is that how Marcus met Natalie Crosby, through Tisha?"

"Natalie knew Marcus?" Allison looked surprised. "Really? I didn't know."

This was not the response Lucky was hoping for. He'd been thinking he'd hit pay dirt. Really, who would know better than an ex-roommate of Tisha's?

"Yeah, I think Natalie knew Marcus. We, the family, are still trying to put together the last few months of his life. He wasn't at home. We're not sure where he was staying. Guess it wasn't here."

"No," Travis said. "I'd have known if he was here."

Lucky's food arrived. He really wasn't hungry, but Texas hospitality would keep the Needhams with him as long as he was eating, and he had a lot more questions. He took a bite and said, "They look alike, Tisha and Natalie."

"That's 'bout all," Travis said. "Natalie's lived here all her life. Tisha just came for summers. All the guys liked Tisha."

"They like Natalie, too?"

"It was a different kind of like," Allison said, looking at Lucky with suspicion. It was definitely time to change the subject.

"What happened to Natalie's leg?" Lucky asked.

Fred answered this one. "The rodeo. All the girls, Allison, Natalie, even Tisha, were into barrel racing."

"Natalie was great," Allison said. "When we were fifteen,

she could do the clover in twenty seconds. No one else could. Sure made Tisha mad."

"She fell during the rodeo you just competed in," Fred said. "Her horse went right and she went left. She landed on one of the barrels. We didn't know how bad it was until later."

"She finished the school semester in a wheelchair," Allison added.

"A few months later," Fred continued, "her dad sold all the horses. Natalie hasn't ridden since."

Lucky pushed his plate away. All that was left was a few crumbs. "She have a boyfriend?"

"Why, you interested?" Allison asked.

The table grew silent, and Lucky shook his head. "Just curious."

Fred pulled out his wallet and placed some money on the table. "Right now, Natalie doesn't need any more complications. Not with her dad so recently deceased." He looked at Lucky. "You do what? Way more than a hundred rodeos a year? Do you even remember the name of the last girl you paid attention to?"

This conversation had definitely taken a turn Lucky wasn't prepared for. He opened his mouth, but no words came out. Fred took that as an answer. Then, he stood and looked at Allison. "It's about time to set the babysitter free. What say we head home?"

Allison stood, looking relieved, shot Lucky a look he couldn't read and followed her dad out the door.

"I take it Natalie's a touchy subject?"

Travis just shook his head. "Not usually, but her father died just a few weeks ago, and some are saying he was having money troubles. Dad thinks she's in danger of losing her home."

"What about Robby's father? Is he helping?"

"No one knows who Robby's father is."

Later, Lucky stared out the window of Mary's room at a full moon. He didn't get along well with his father, never had, but Lucky couldn't imagine his dad suddenly being *gone*. Lucky should have asked more questions about Natalie's family. He weighed his options. Child support, money for Marcus's son was no problem, but it would certainly come with strings. His parents, especially his mother, would want to be involved in the child's life. There were also aunts, uncles, cousins, friends…

Lucky's last thought, before drifting off to sleep, was just how Marcus had kept this a secret and why?

Natalie stretched. All morning she'd battled fatigue and stress, and wouldn't you know it, she'd done some of her best work. Glancing at the printout, she then looked at the screen, checked all the spelling and once again made sure the video trailer she'd created took only seconds to load.

She usually didn't get to work this late in the morning. Usually, by now, she was watching *The Wiggles* with Robby. She'd been lucky seven years ago, when she'd created a Web site in a high school computer class. The teacher liked her design and introduced her to his wife, who'd started designing Web pages as a stay-at-home job. Natalie and she became business partners. When Natalie got older and her partner had two more children, Natalie took over the business and it grew.

It had paid for college so that her father didn't have to. It had helped support her and Robby. But it hadn't covered everything. Natalie needed to gain more clients now.

"Mommy, milk."

"Sure, Robby. When did you wake up?"

"When my eyes opened."

She pushed the laptop toward the middle of the table and

stood. Julia Child had nothing to worry about. Natalie's idea of a good breakfast was a pancake she could pop in the microwave and a cold glass of milk.

Robby, a boy of few words in the morning, got himself a plate and paper towel, and then climbed up on Pop Pop's chair and waited.

A minute later, the newspaper hit the front door and the pancakes were ready.

Robby got the paper; Natalie set the food out.

The front page of the *Selena Gazette* featured the rodeo, make that the rodeo star.

A bit of pancake lodged in Natalie's throat. She tried to swallow, but coughed. Half of her glass of milk soaked the front of her shirt; the other half splashed onto the floor. She quickly grabbed a rag. Usually, it was Robby's spilled milk. Unlike her, he didn't cry over the mess. But then, she really wasn't crying about the milk.

After a moment, she sat back at the table and stared at Monday's newspaper. There he was. A winner. The picture had been taken yesterday, as Lucky conducted something called Cowboy Church. Standing next to him, with admiration written on her face, was a local girl, a Realtor's daughter.

She'd expected Lucky to show up yesterday. It had taken every ounce of courage not to turn off the lights, shut the curtains and move heavy furniture in front of the door. But instead of showing up at her door, the Big Bad Wolf had been at church.

She glanced at the newspaper article. Cowboy Church? Okay, maybe Big Bad Wolf was an unfair moniker. And, in truth, she'd started this fiasco—she and her big mouth.

Lucky had looked shocked by her announcement—and her demand.

Even from the grainy black-and-white picture, Natalie could see what made him more than a typical cowboy. He had a magnetism that upset her stomach. She wanted to blame the pancake, but in all honesty, it was Lucky who sent the butterflies fluttering in her stomach.

Natalie had wondered all along if Marcus hadn't told his family. That would explain why they'd left her alone. Until her dad's death, she hadn't cared, really, hadn't needed help or money.

She should have waited, thought this through, not acted on impulse. Of course, impulse was what brought Robby into her life.

Robby slurped the last of his milk. "I'm finished," he announced, pushing away the plate. In a moment, he was out of the chair, into the living room and back in the kitchen wearing Pop Pop's cowboy hat. Too big, it had the habit of falling in Robby's eyes, and he whipped it off and let out a whoop. Since yesterday, he'd continually ridden a broom around the house. Even worse, he'd gotten really good at pretending to fall off.

He hit the ground, pure rodeo landing, and she flinched.

Pop Pop would have had the video camera out.

What had Natalie been thinking?

She hadn't!

The loss of her father and the muddle of his finances must have rendered her temporarily insane. It was the only explanation for her behavior.

Robby galloped back into the room. "Mommy, go park?"

Natalie nodded. "We'll go to the bank, and then to the park."

That was good enough for Robby. He dismounted, carefully guided his broom horse to lean against the oven and ran to get his favorite train. After she'd cleared up the dishes and zipped Robby into his jacket, they were out the door and heading toward town.

Selena had one bank. Its claim to fame wasn't beauty. It was as rectangular as a cracker box and too small for the town. But change came slowly to Selena and not even the town's most forward-thinking seemed inclined to fix what wasn't really broken.

Mondays were busy, which explained why Natalie managed to get past the tellers without chitchat.

Unfortunately, Robby wasn't about to miss an opportunity.

"Hi, Allie," Robby chirped.

Allison Needham grinned at him, still counting money without missing a beat.

"Morning, Allison," Natalie said. On top of everything else, Natalie always worried that maybe Allison knew a bit too much. After all, she'd been Tisha's friend back when Tisha came to Selena to spend summers. Then, later, when Allison decided to give rodeoing a shot, she'd followed after Tisha, who was giving rodeoing a different kind of shot.

Just as Natalie walked toward the bank president's office, Walter Hughes came out of it. Seven years ago, it had been his office. Now, it was his son's. He stopped when he saw Natalie, handed Robby a peppermint from his pocket and said, "You need anything, little girl?"

"I'm hoping your son has a few minutes to give me."

Timothy Hughes, who'd sat across from Natalie in almost every class in grade school, and who'd been her first high school crush, came to the door. "Natalie? Come on in."

Walter looked at his son and Timothy nodded. "You mind if I sit in?" Walter asked.

Her eyes started pooling. Walt had thinning gray hair, like Dad. He wore the same kind of casual clothes. He still opened doors for women, and he made her miss her father all over again.

"No, not a bit."

"Let me pull Allison away from the front," Timothy said. "She can watch Robby for a few minutes."

Robby willingly took Allison's hand, and Allison headed out the front door and down the sidewalk. Robby loved to walk. He could walk up and down the street for hours, seeing the same sights, saying "hi" to the same people, and never get bored.

It took a few minutes for Timothy to gather the files and punch up her information on the computer. Walter chewed his bottom lip and perused a copy of her father's will. Yesterday, while Robby napped, she'd spent two hours itemizing what she had, what she didn't have and what she was unsure about. She'd gone over the will in detail and listed her tangible property. Now, she had very specific questions. Timothy couldn't answer her concern about the life insurance, but he could show how a good deal of money had gone into a new roof, new air-conditioning and taxes. After playing with the numbers, what she had and what she could earn, he agreed with her assessment. She could make it about three months.

Walter was the one with questions. "I think I know all of your dad's tangible personal property, and I'm as surprised as you are that he used the business as collateral for a loan, but, Natalie, were there deeds to any other properties?"

"None, and I would have known."

"And insurance?"

"The only one I found paid for his funeral."

Timothy's face finally changed expression. "Are you sure there's not something in your dad's safe-deposit box? Could you have missed seeing the policy?"

Natalie gripped the arms of the chair. She'd been so careful with the paperwork, with what was in the house. "I didn't even know he had a safe-deposit box. I certainly don't have the key."

Hope, Natalie started feeling a dim hope. It made her sit taller, but only for a moment, because the feeling of hope was just as quickly followed by fear. Why hadn't she known about the box? What if it was empty? Or what if it just held some of her mother's jewelry—worth a little but not a lot.

Still, hope flared a bit. What if the missing funds were somehow accounted for inside the safe-deposit box?

Then she'd have involved the Welch family for nothing.

"Think you can find the key?" Timothy interrupted her scrambled thoughts.

"I—"

"We're not messing with that," Walter said. "I'll make a call. We'll drill it open in no time."

"Dad, that costs almost a hundred—"

"Exactly what we should pay for not notifying Natalie about the safe-deposit box sooner."

An hour later, Natalie knew that approaching Lucky Welch for money was, indeed, the last thing she should have done. Her dad had kept his promise in the form of bank bonds, *lots* of bank bonds. Barring a catastrophe, they had enough to stay afloat for two to three years, not even counting Natalie's income.

It did raise a few questions while still leaving others unanswered. Natalie still didn't know why her father had cleaned out the checking account or borrowed against his half of the business.

"Mommy, we go park now?" Robby was at the office door, Allison behind him.

"It's like having Jasmin come visit me at work," Allison said. Her daughter was only a little older than Robby. "She loves to walk, too."

"Thanks, Allison," Walter said. "Natalie, I'm thinking you need some cash now. Would you like to turn in a few bonds and then maybe meet with your dad's financial advisor about what to do with the rest?"

Natalie could only nod.

Her money troubles were over *for now,* but she had new troubles and they were by no means over and *may never be.*

"Mommy, we go now?"

Natalie was more than ready to *go now.* And the park was the best destination. Home was too empty.

Twenty minutes later, feelings raw, she watched Robby at play. He had changed her whole life.

Amazingly so.

And all because she'd been home alone on a Friday night, studying for a math test.

She hadn't even known Tisha was pregnant, let alone that she'd given birth. That Friday night, after her initial shock, she'd thought she was saying yes to helping out, watching a tiny, two-week-old Robby for a night. Truthfully, she'd loved sitting in her little apartment a mile away from New Mexico State University and watching the little guy sleep. She'd unfortunately figured out by the next evening that the phone number Tisha left was wrong, that formula and diapers were expensive and that nobody—including Tisha's parents—knew where Tisha was.

She skipped the next two days of school and her dad had driven to Las Cruces. He'd stayed a week. With his help, she'd found a sitter for the remaining month of school, and by the time the semester ended, she'd realized what it felt like to be separated from Robby, like she could still feel the warmth of his little body in the crook of her left arm. It had taken her from the hallways of higher academia and back home to walking the hallways with a little personality who liked to touch her cheek and who smiled—yes, smiled—at the whole world.

Soon, her dad felt the same way, and they'd stopped looking for Tisha.

When the whole town assumed Natalie was Robby's mama, Natalie and her dad had gone along. At the time, it was easier than explaining, and Natalie didn't want Robby to ever see the kind of look that passed between judgmental adults whenever Tisha's name was mentioned.

Natalie had been an only child and had always wanted brothers and sisters. Her cousin Tisha had been the closest thing to a sibling, and Natalie loved her—flaws and all—even if she didn't always like Tisha or the choices she made.

Tisha at first claimed she didn't know who Robby's father was. A year later, when Tisha borrowed some money from Natalie, she'd mentioned Marcus.

She'd also mentioned Marcus's dad and how strict he was, how he always got what he wanted.

Natalie swallowed. Here she sat on her nice, safe bench while Robby played. Maybe the park was the only safe place. At home, there was the newspaper article featuring Lucky. She'd have to deal with her mistake. Figure out the right thing to do. What was right for Robby.

Maybe Lucky would saddle up and ride away. Yeah, right. Truth was, if what Natalie knew about Lucky was true, soon he'd probably be out on the playground, climbing the jungle gym, and teaching Robby how to do something dangerous like jump.

That's what her dad would have had done. It's what he'd done for Natalie. After her mother died, he'd swallowed his sorrow and stepped right into the role of both parents. He cooked dinner, went on field trips and even sat through ballet lessons. Of course, she only took the lessons after he convinced her that the grace of a ballet dancer would benefit a barrel racer.

Her dad had always taken care of her.

He'd taught her to jump, and he'd made sure she always had a soft place to fall.

Natalie swallowed. Robby, brown hair tussled by the wind and an unguarded grin on his face—was jumping just fine. He climbed the slide, slid down, got to the bottom, stood up and jumped. Then, he tried to climb up the slide instead of the steps. He fell, skidded and hit the ground. Natalie started to get up, wanting to cushion his fall, but Robby didn't need help. He managed on his own. Standing, climbing, falling and laughing the whole time. He was all boy.

Thanks to her father, she could take care of herself and Robby.

It was her own fault she had to deal with the Welches.

Chapter Three

Sunday had been pretty much a blur for Lucky. Otherwise, he'd never have allowed a photographer to take pictures after the morning service. What he did on the circuit could be sensationalized. What he did on Sunday morning in front of believers should not.

The girl in the photo was wearing next to nothing. And the adoring look she aimed his way was rehearsed. Luckily, the reporter knew how to gather facts: Lucky's rodeo win, his mother's rodeo-queen status, his brother's rodeo belts and recent death, and even Lucky's penchant for sermonizing, all made it into the story. Too bad God was at the bottom of the pyramid. The reporter definitely put the facts in the wrong order of importance.

God should have been first.

Lucky got out his Bible and turned to James. *"Every good and perfect gift is from above, coming down from the Father of the heavenly lights, who does not change like shifting shadows."*

He put his hand flat on the page. Sometimes, in the quiet of the early morning and in the twilight of the night, when

Lucky was alone, the touch of the Bible felt like a pathway straight to God.

He reread the passage. To Lucky's way of thinking, no matter what Marcus had done or been, Robby Crosby was a good and perfect gift. One Lucky's mother would welcome and his father would shun.

Lucky closed the Bible, held it in his hands and stared out his window. It was just after five. Howard, Bernice's husband, was already taking care of the animals. Howie Junior should be with him. Those summers when Lucky and Marcus visited Grandpa and Grandma Moody, they'd been up at five.

Finally setting his Bible aside, Lucky started dialing the numbers in his cell phone. He'd devoted yesterday to God, prayer and meditation. Today he was devoting to Robby Crosby, who maybe needed to be known as Robby Welch. Surely, out of all the friends he and Marcus shared, somebody would know something. Two hours later, he lost the charge on his cell phone, switched to the landline in Mary's room, and he discovered what he'd suspected all along. Natalie obviously kept a low profile. No one seemed to know her or remember Marcus talking about her. Everyone remembered Tisha. And, like Lucky, most agreed that she had stopped following the rodeo after she stopped seeing Marcus.

No one had seen her in the last few years.

No one cared.

During the time she'd spent with Marcus, Lucky had felt displaced and his youthful prayers about her all had to do with her disappearing. He'd hated when Tisha accompanied them from one show to another. She'd been a wedge between him and his brother. He was older now, and maybe his prayers should take a different slant.

Marcus had probably been a father, and it looked like he had a son to be proud of. A tiny seed of suspicion settled in

Lucky's gut. Could Marcus have cheated on Tisha with this Natalie woman? Or could Natalie have been a rebound because she looked so much like Tisha?

Either scenario might give some insight as to why Marcus had kept his son a secret.

Lucky headed for the kitchen and the beckoning aroma of pancakes. "Bernice!"

"I'm right here. You don't need to yell. What?" Bernice wore an apron over her jeans as she expertly flipped the pancakes while holding a gallon of milk in her other hand. "Don't tell me you're not staying for breakfast."

"I'm staying and I'm starved. Do you know Natalie Crosby?"

"Sure I know Natalie, ever since she was a little girl." Bernice looked at Lucky's mother. "You'd know Natalie's mama. Tina Burke. She was a freshman when we were seniors."

Betsy Welch shook her head. "I don't remember."

Bernice shook her head. "About the time your daddy died and the boys stopped coming here for the summer, that would be about the time Natalie started performing in the rodeo. About a summer or two later, Tisha started coming for the summers and got involved. It's a wonder that Tisha and Marcus met elsewhere—both of them have roots here." She patted Betsy on the shoulder before turning to Lucky. "I heard you burning up the phone line asking questions about that girl. I could have saved Marcus a passel of trouble if he'd listened when I told him she was nothing but trouble."

Lucky looked at his mother. She'd poured herself a cup of coffee and was taking a seat at the table. She didn't even glance at the plate of pancakes in front of her. The look on her face clearly indicated she knew something bad was about to happen. The name Tisha always had that effect on his mother.

"Did Marcus know Natalie?" Lucky asked.

"Not that I know of." Bernice set the milk on the counter. "You want to tell me why you're asking?"

"I met Natalie yesterday at the rodeo and, for a moment, I thought she was Tisha. Some of her friends quickly set me straight."

"Natalie was at the rodeo?" Bernice sounded surprised.

"Yes."

"Well, that's interesting. After her leg got mangled so bad, Natalie stopped going anywhere near horses. Her father sold off his entire stock. About broke his heart. When Robby started wearing a cowboy hat, you could just see Leo wishing he had a horse to put that boy on."

"You're not looking for Tisha, are you?" his mother asked slowly.

"It really shocked me, Mom, how much this Natalie looked like Tisha." Lucky sat down at the table and tried not to notice his mother's trembling hands. Tisha brought up bad memories. Marcus's drinking had gotten out of control during the Tisha era. His mom blamed Tisha, slightly unfair, but not completely unwarranted.

Bernice piled pancakes on a plate and set them in front of him. His mother stared at the syrup bottle in front of her but didn't move. Finally, Bernice reached over and pushed it toward Lucky. "Don't worry, Betsy. Natalie's nothing like Tisha."

Betsy wiped away a tear, and Bernice started talking, even as she dug into her own plate of pancakes. "Everyone loves Natalie. She's a hometown girl. Family's been here since the area was first settled."

Bernice looked at Lucky. "At one time, that girl loved the rodeo as much as you do. Of course, Tisha did, too. My, my, those two girls could ride, but Natalie was a natural. She and little Allison Needham used to practice every weekend. I heard you asking questions about her, too, didn't I? My Mary said she wouldn't be surprised if Natalie made a name for herself. She wasn't too sure about Allison. I think Tisha only rode because she couldn't bear Natalie getting the attention. When Natalie was still a teenager, she got tossed during the rodeo. She was still using a cane when she graduated high school. If you look real close, you'll see she still has a limp to this day."

"I think I saw her," Betsy said thoughtfully, looking at Lucky and finally relaxing. "She came over to talk to you after the rodeo."

"Yeah, she did."

"I only saw her from the back. I didn't notice she looked like Tisha."

"Her boy must have convinced her to bring him. Can't think of anything else that would get her there. She's a good mother. Too bad there's not a dad in the picture. She went off to college and came back two years later with a little baby. Leo didn't even blink, and no one dared say a word or ask questions about Natalie's situation. She and her dad dote, make that he doted, on Robby." Bernice looked over at Betsy. "Natalie's father died just two weeks ago. Heart attack. Real surprise to everyone."

Bernice turned to Lucky. "Natalie's dad owned part of the stockyard Howard works at. We all expected to hear that Natalie would take over the reins, but it seems just a few months ago, Leo took out a loan. He used the stockyard as collateral. It's gone now, Natalie's livelihood. Word is, she's hurting for money and might lose her home."

Lucky nodded. So desperation drove her to him. That she'd risk talking to him, asking him for child support, for help, meant she was pretty much at wit's end financially. No doubt she wanted money with no strings. He finished his plate and wasn't surprised when Bernice piled more on.

With each bite, he thought of his brother. Marcus had been a pro at keeping secrets from his family. He'd spent time in jail without placing his one phone call to them. He'd nursed an alcohol addiction that not even Alcoholics Anonymous had been able to counter. But of all his secrets, this one took the prize.

Then, a more subtle thought surfaced, adding one more turn on this roller-coaster ride out of control. Maybe Marcus hadn't known he was a father?

Suddenly Lucky's appetite was gone. "Where does Natalie live?"

"Three blocks past the church, turn right and go down Judge Taylor Road all the way to the end."

He stood. "I need to get going."

They didn't ask; he didn't tell.

He rehearsed his speech on the drive over, in between praying. There were two possible scenarios. One, Natalie was a decent woman who truly needed help. Lucky had watched decent women fall victim to Marcus. Two, Natalie was the same as Tisha. Then, possibly, Marcus had been the victim.

No matter which one she was, approaching her looked to be the hardest thing Lucky had ever done. The words he practiced seemed weak, hollow, accusing. As he pulled in front of the house, he was no closer to knowing what to say to the mother of Marcus's child.

Sitting in his truck in the driveway, Lucky bowed his head and one last time petitioned his Father. Never had he dealt with such a situation. He couldn't even come up with a Bible reference.

Natalie came to the door, stared at Lucky, disappeared inside for a moment, then stepped onto the porch. He admired that. She wasn't going to hide. She'd meet him head-on. He also had to admire the way she looked. White jeans, red button-down shirt. Perky and mad. On her, the combination looked good.

The boy wriggled up next to her. Grinning like it was Christmas and obviously hoping for escape. The tears Lucky evoked yesterday obviously forgotten.

Thank you, God.

Lucky stepped out of his truck. "Ma'am, can we talk?"

"Robby, go up to your room." She slipped her hands into the back pockets of her jeans and frowned.

"Why, Mommy?"

"Just for a little while. I'll talk to you later."

The boy peeked out. "Are you the cowboy?"

"I'm a bull rider," Lucky corrected, throwing an apologetic look to Natalie. "A cowboy *and a bull rider,* much better."

"Better?" The boy looked interested.

"Robby." The one word did it. Robby bobbed his head, grinned and ducked behind her.

"I wanted to talk to you—" Lucky began.

"I owe you an apology," Natalie said. "I'm not sure what came over me yesterday. It was a mistake to come see you. We don't need money. Really."

Lucky shook his head. "Ma'am, we can worry about money later. Right now, I just want to know how it can be that my brother had a son the family doesn't know about."

She stumbled, then stopped to lean against one of the porch's white pillars. Suddenly, he wanted to go to her. Hold her up. Tell her he didn't mean to hurt her. Where were these feelings coming from? This morning, with the sun hitting the blond, almost white, highlights in her hair, she looked nothing like Tisha.

"So, you didn't know," she whispered before regaining her footing.

She drew herself up, standing proud, yet still whispering. "I always wondered."

"Ma'am, we had no idea. When I tell my mother about Robby, she's going to be so happy. I cannot even tell you how much that little boy will heal our family. I know we can work something—"

"No!" She took two slow steps down the front steps. The limp was more pronounced, as if the emotional pain robbed her physically as well as mentally. Still, she managed to keep steady. "I was so wrong to approach you. Robby and I are doing just fine."

"I believe you, ma'am. I can see how fine you're doing. Little Robby looks happy and healthy, and this is a great spread you got here, but *I'm* not doing fine. For six months, I've done nothing but miss my brother, wish I could bring him back, and now I find out he has a son—a son who knows nothing about his father or his father's family? Tell me, ma'am, did Marcus know about Robby? Did you tell him?"

"Tell him? Why would *I* tell him?" The look in her eyes said it all. Marcus was pond scum. "We, my father and I, wanted nothing to do with Marcus, ever. We were glad he never came around. Robby's ours. We kept him, we love him, and he's ours. And keep your voice down. He doesn't know he's related to you."

"That's going to change. Robby has family, on both sides, who want to get to know him and love him."

Natalie's eyes narrowed.

"By not telling my brother about Robby, you deprived him of any opportunity to know his son." Lucky felt the words pool in his throat. Maybe knowing he had a son would have calmed Marcus down, grounded him, made him rethink what he did with his time and his money. "I know my brother. He would have taken care of Robby."

"No," Natalie said.

"Look, how and when did you meet him? What made you decide to raise his child alone? Why…"

She covered her ears. The pain on her face so evident that Lucky stopped.

"I can't deal with this right now," she said.

He started to argue, but tears pooled in her eyes and threatened to overflow.

"It's too much. I've dealt with losing my dad, losing my home, and now you're making me deal with losing Robby."

"No, not losing Robby, but introducing—"

She held up her hand. "No, not today, I cannot deal with this today." She took one step in his direction, and he backed up. He recognized anguish. He'd felt it every day since his brother died. Their eyes locked, hers blue and beautiful, then she pivoted and hurried quickly back to her front door.

A moment later, sitting in his truck in the driveway again, Lucky bowed his head once more and petitioned his Father, even as his heart pounded and his own anguish threatened to take over. He'd finally thought of a Bible reference. The story of King Solomon offering to cut a child in half when two women were arguing over who was the infant's rightful family.

When he looked up from his prayer, his eyes went right back to Natalie Crosby.

She stood at the front door, looking at him like he was either the Grim Reaper or an IRS agent.

Finally, he rolled down the window and leaned out. The smell of West Texas sage grass reminded him of being at his grandparents' house. Lord, he could use Grandpa's advice now. "Look, Natalie, you know you're going to wind up talking to me. I've got plenty of questions and seems you're the only one who can answer them." He shook his head.

"Saturday you told me that I'm an uncle. Surely after that bombshell, you know I'm not going away."

Her expression didn't change. He'd dealt with friendlier bulls.

"Okay," he finally said. "The next time we talk, it probably won't be you and me. It will be you and me and my lawyer." The next words out of his mouth shamed him, but she'd left him no choice. "And I don't think you can afford that."

He fired the engine and backed out. Just when he hit the street, he paused, stuck his head out the window again, because he couldn't stand feeling this low, and shouted, "I'm staying at Bernice Baker's place. You can call me anytime. I know you can find her number."

With that, he pointed his truck toward Bernice's, but his white knuckles and clenched teeth convinced him that no way, no how, could he sit in Bernice's living room and not look like something was wrong. Holing up in Mary's bedroom wouldn't work, either. He was driving away from one headache and heading toward another. He needed to tell his family, and soon. Because if they found out about Robby from someone else, he'd never hear the end of it.

Selena in November was a riot of colors. The trees were shades of orange, red and yellow. The grass was turning brown but still had hints of green. None of the scenery matched Lucky's mood. He needed some black or at least a lot more brown. He drove out of town and headed toward Delaney. Maybe there he could recover some feeling of peace.

Delaney was even smaller than Selena and just as colorful. A small sign announced the town and its population. An even smaller sign pointed to a café and general store. Both were new. School was in session. The building, the same size as the combined café and general store, had four trucks and one Ford Taurus parked in front. Lucky turned at the corner and saw a playground much improved since the days he had climbed the metal slide or fallen onto dirt and grass from the monkey bars. He still wasn't seeing the colors that fit his mood. While the playground of old had been brown, green and silver, the playground of new was sunny yellow and fire-engine red.

Down from the school was the church his grandparents attended. It still looked good; getting declared a historical marker had that effect on property. Lucky pulled into the parking lot and almost couldn't get out of the truck. The church looked good but lonely. The minister who'd been there during his grandparents' time had passed away five years ago.

The sight of his childhood church looking pristine but unused did not help Lucky's mood.

He left Delaney's few businesses and traveled five miles of dirt roads, finally reaching his grandfather's house. He stopped just in front and let his foot hover over the gas as he reflected back on the best memories of his life. A discarded bike, a tiny pretend lawn mower and a wagon gave evidence that life indeed went on. Lucky didn't know the family who'd purchased Grandpa's land, but he liked them already. The place looked pretty much as it always had, even the horses running in the distance. The only thing missing was the carpet-covered barrels over by the barn and Grandma standing on the porch yelling at Grandpa to turn down the music so she could think.

Believe it or not, Grandpa said there was nothing like Jimi Hendrix to get the adrenaline pumping. He said it was necessary for bull riding.

Lucky relaxed enough so his knuckles returned to their normal color.

The cemetery was a good twenty miles away and one of the oldest and biggest in the area. He'd been to Grandpa's grave often, every time the rodeo brought him near, but today the pull was more than paying respect. It was a place to reflect.

He certainly could have handled his encounter with Natalie better this morning.

And it looked like he'd need to work hard to handle his mother now. In the distance he could see her standing in front of her parents' graves. On a patch of land that usually inspired the wearing of black, his mother wore a pink button-down dress and white high heels. Yup, she was an avid member of the June Cleaver fan club. At least that's what his friends all claimed. No one ever surprised Betsy Welch in an awkward moment. She always looked like she'd just left the hairdresser.

He parked alongside a Virgin Mary statue. The cemetery didn't have a fence surrounding it. To the best of Lucky's knowledge, the need to escape Delaney ended at the grave. It took him only a minute to join his mother in front of her parents' graves. The headstones were weathered yet dignified. A Bible verse was engraved under his grandfather's name:

Thomas William Hitch
1917–1999
He followed the Lord.

"We should have buried Marcus here." Her voice broke. "I don't know what your father was thinking. My family's here. The cemetery back in Houston is full of strangers."

"Mom, it's okay. Marcus really doesn't care where he's buried."

"But I care! And I should have brought flowers today."

There was a grave, fairly new, just one row up. The wealth of flowers stacked there caught the sunshine. Another wasted life? Or did the grave, like Lucky's grandfather's, denote he followed the Lord?

Lucky took his mother by the elbow and started leading her away. "We can come out again."

"I checked out that grave over there," his mother said.

"The one with the flowers?"

"Yes."

"Did you know that person?"

"No, but Bernice mentioned him this morning. Leo Crosby."

Lucky slowed his pace. "Natalie's father? Wonder why he's buried here instead of in Selena?"

"I checked around. There are lots of Crosby graves, some from as early as 1862."

"Hold on, Mom. I want to go take a look."

A moment later, staring down at Leonard Crosby's headstone, Lucky reassessed his day. He'd thought he'd come here for conversation with God and Grandpa. Instead, he got his mother and now Leo Crosby, who was lying under a covering of not only flowers, but also a brown teddy bear with a toy train nestled between its legs.

Maybe his mother was right. Maybe if Marcus were buried here, he'd have flowers on his grave and maybe even a little toy train.

He knew what his mother wanted—someone to listen, someone to understand and someone to grieve with her, someone to fill a void. Since his brother's death, it was the only thing she wanted.

A grandchild would surely comfort her grieving heart.

Chapter Four

Loss of sleep became a way of life over the next few days. Natalie didn't go to town, afraid of confrontation, and she didn't tell Robby the truth, afraid of his desire to know a real cowboy and just how much said cowboy *and his family* could change their lives.

On Friday morning, she took Robby for a walk around the property. It might be mid-November, but he only needed a sweater. West Texas weather was a bit like Robby, sunny one minute, tears the next, and oh, when he was mad, he certainly knew how to freeze a body out. Today, the ranch smelled like sage and felt like Indian summer.

After an hour, they headed back for a snack and some downtime. Okay, Robby wanted the snack; she wanted the downtime. He stomped into the living room and plopped onto the floor. Natalie made sure he was busy with his trains and then walked around the house, turning on lights and trying to ignore the feeling of loss that followed her. Even with Robby's noise, her father's absence was tangible.

His accounting books were still open on the kitchen table. She no longer had so many questions; she had a few answers.

Still, she needed to know what had happened to Dad's share in the business. Why was his checking account wiped out?

Slowly, she took a seat at the kitchen table and flipped open Daddy's checkbook. She should have taken an interest long ago. He'd always told her that he'd make sure she—they—didn't need to worry.

Hey, Dad, I'm worrying here.

She rubbed her finger over the black ink. He had tiny handwriting, always print, and it slanted ridiculously to the right. He'd chase down a penny if his balance didn't add up. Sighing, she pushed away the evidence she couldn't change, at least not at the moment and not in her current frame of mind.

Heading for the living room, she joined Robby on the floor. He'd managed to crawl under the coffee table and was running a little green train across a terrain of brown carpet. She started to get up, but he said, "Stay, Mommy, stay." He could play for hours and loved having her sit right beside him. He didn't want her to play, just to be by his side. Apparently, she hadn't inherited the I-know-how-to-push-trains-across-the-carpet gene. If she reached for one, he would say, "Noooo."

It was okay if Pop Pop reached for one, though, and choo-chooed around the room. And if one of Natalie's or Pop Pop's friends stopped by, they were welcome to play. Just not Natalie. There were other things for her to do, like hold her hand at the ready so Robby didn't bump his head when he finally wriggled out from under the coffee table. Her hand often made the difference between smiles and tears.

There'd been too many tears her hands couldn't prevent lately.

She leaned against the couch and closed her eyes. When she opened them again, Robby remained happily entertained, sprawled under the coffee table. Natalie stared at the photographs hanging on the living room wall. The earliest showed the ranch as it looked in 1910, with lots of brush and dirt, four cowboys, two dogs and six horses. Natalie didn't know if the building in the background was the beginnings of the ranch or an outhouse.

The newest photo, one taken by her father, showed a ranch with trees and lots of green grass, no cowboys, no dogs and, since her accident, no horses. The house—white, sprawling and two-storied—had two chairs on the porch and Robby's tricycle on the path.

The phone rang loud, unwelcome and jarring. She'd left it off the hook too often lately. Condolences from those who had loved her father seemed to deepen her sorrow, not relieve it. Then, there was Lucky Welch, the bull rider who was staying with the Bakers, who knew where she lived and who could definitely find her phone number.

She let it ring. Maybe he'd go away. Maybe hiding out was working. But she couldn't hide for long. The postman knew where she lived. Robby heard the sound of the mail truck. He loved the postman, who often had peppermints in his pockets.

"Mama!" Robby was at the door and twisting the knob before she made it off the floor. She needn't have hurried. The postman was out of his truck and coming up the walk.

"You got something official," he said. "Probably about your daddy."

Natalie took the envelope, the official-looking envelope, and stared at the return address.

She couldn't breathe.

She couldn't swallow, either.

Opening the screen door, she wandered onto the front porch and collapsed in a wooden rocker. The smooth wood creaked under her weight, or maybe it creaked because she held the weight of the world upon her shoulders.

How had it all gone so wrong?

And though it was the last thing she wanted to do, she went inside and opened the envelope. Inside was a single sheet on fancy letterhead. She'd been right to berate herself for a fool-hardy action, right to worry about a custody battle, right to wonder what kind of man Lucky Welch was.

He wasn't his brother, that was for sure. No, instead, Lucky got things done.

Attending the rodeo and approaching Lucky had been stupid. She'd done this on her own. With no help from anyone else, she'd made her life a soap opera. Suddenly, losing her home didn't seem such a disaster, not when she compared it to losing Robby.

The lawyer's letter was straightforward. Lucas William Welch requested a meeting. The letter suggested it be in Selena. Lucky's lawyer would travel here, and it specified a date and a time next week. If the date and time were not convenient, she was instructed to call.

With trembling hands, she laid the letter on the kitchen table and looked into the living room where Robby busied himself by pounding on the coffee table with a toy train.

"Robby, stop!"

He looked at her, looked at the train, and then gently tapped it on the coffee table.

For the past three days, she'd been faced with a curious child and no words to explain what had happened. Robby had so many questions. Who was the cowboy and why did he come to the house? Why was Mommy crying all the time? Why couldn't he go to a friend's house? She'd settled for telling Robby that she didn't feel well, and that the rodeo brought back old memories and so did Lucky. It wasn't a complete truth, but it certainly wasn't a lie, either.

Oh, what had she done?

For the last three days, instead of holing up, she should have been busy finding herself a lawyer because no way could she bear to lose Robby, especially so soon after her father's death, or any other time, for that matter.

Selena had two lawyers. One had been her father's. He was old-fashioned and spent more time patting Natalie on the hand when she asked questions about her dad's money than he had investigating where the money had gone. Sunni Foreman was brand-new to the community and trying to make a dent in what had always been, at least in Selena, a man's world. A quick phone call got Natalie an afternoon appointment. A second phone call arranged for Patty to watch Robby. Robby was more than ready for an afternoon of play with other kids, and he didn't even cry when she left him.

Sunni Foreman shared office space with an accountant and a wedding planner. They didn't share a secretary. Natalie noticed that the waiting room was clean and had current magazines. The chairs looked new and, before she could knock, Ms. Foreman, as the plaque on the door read, stuck her head out of her office and said, "Come on in."

The good news was that everything happened so fast that before Natalie could get nervous, she was sitting in a comfortable maroon chair in an office with a picture of George Washington on the wall and the scent of cinnamon apples all around. Ms. Foreman started to sit down, then left the room for a moment. "Call me Sunni," the lawyer said when she returned, bringing Natalie a glass of water.

Sunni stood over six feet tall, had frizzy blond hair that certainly deserved the woman's moniker, and wore a white top with a blue jacket over a pair of well-worn blue jeans. Natalie had seen her around town at the grocery store, the library and such. She wasn't the type of woman likely to be missed.

Opening her purse, Natalie handed Sunni the letter.

Sunni sat at her desk, reached for glasses and held them instead of putting them on. "Before I read this, why don't you, in your own words, tell me what's going on."

Natalie took a drink of the cold water. Setting the glass down carefully, Natalie took a breath, and the words poured out of her so fast they tumbled right over each other. She started with her father's death, the money situation and the mistake at the rodeo, then went on to finding out she did have money, and finally arrived at Lucky's visit to the ranch and the letter Sunni was holding.

When she finished, she almost felt better, but not quite. Her father's death wasn't the beginning, and with her lawyer, she needed to start at the beginning.

Tisha showing up at Natalie's place in New Mexico, a tiny baby in her arms, was the real beginning.

Sunni opened the letter from Lucky's lawyer and read. After a moment she said, "Seems pretty straightforward. By your own admission, Marcus Welch is the father. His family does deserve visitation, and you are the one who initiated contact. Tell me what you want out of this upcoming meeting."

"I—I want it so that nothing changes."

"That's a pretty broad request and judging by this letter, it's not an option."

Reaching down, Natalie put her hand in her purse and curled her fingers around a stiff manila envelope. She didn't bring it out, couldn't yet, because she didn't want to cry, didn't want to acknowledge the fear threatening to spill over.

The tick, tick, tick of the office's plain brown clock seemed to get louder before Sunni, who looked at Natalie like she could see right into her soul, gently continued. "Is there any reason to deny them a chance to get to know Robby? Fathers, and their families, have rights. Unless you're worried they might abduct Robby, I don't see why you need me. My best advice is to call this Lucas Welch, apologize for how you ended his last contact and ask if you can meet without lawyers."

Natalie swallowed. Nowhere in the television shows about lawyers, the books she'd read about lawyers and in the dealings she'd witnessed with her dad's lawyer had she heard the words...*without lawyers*. Well, she'd wanted an honest lawyer; looked like she'd found one.

Natalie's fingers still curled around the envelope. Now, she tightened her grip and slowly brought the envelope to the desk. "There's a reason why I need a lawyer and a reason why I don't want this meeting with the Welches." Leaning forward, Natalie asked the question that she most dreaded hearing the answer to. "Anything we discuss in here is private, privileged, right?"

"Yes." The lawyer waited silently, as if knowing Natalie needed time to regroup. Silence was a type of pressure.

"Well, um, the letter instructed me to bring one thing. Robby's birth certificate."

"Do you have it?"

"I do."

Before Natalie could change her mind, Sunni Foreman's hand reached across the desk and Natalie relinquished the packet.

Inside was a copy of Robby's birth certificate. Sunni pulled that out first, glanced at it, glanced at Natalie, and then pulled out the rest of the papers. After a moment, she looked at Natalie again. "Okay, I see your dilemma. What is it you hope I can do for you?"

"I can't negotiate any rights for Robby," Natalie said. "I can't sign any paperwork. But I want, I deserve, to be the one who calls the shots. That little boy is mine, and I want what's best for him."

"And you're what's best for Robby?" Sunni asked.

"I am."

Sunni nodded, leaned forward and said, "You've got no ammunition here, nothing to help your case, not even guardianship papers. Marcus's family will have the law on their side. You knew Marcus was the father but never informed him, so basically, you've been raising his son without his knowledge or permission."

"But Tisha—"

"Abandoned her son."

"I took him when no one wanted him."

"Don't even begin to go with that argument." Sunni tapped the letter from Lucky's lawyer. "This is just the first step in a long walk that leads to how many people want Robby."

"I…" Natalie stopped talking. Tears dripped down her nose. She'd spent more time crying this last month than she had her whole life, including when her dad sold off all the horses.

Sunni waited, her face a neutral mask of professionalism. It was just what Natalie needed. Tears didn't win wars; lawyers did.

"What do we do first?" Natalie finally said, bracing herself. She had no clue what advice the lawyer would give. She just hoped there would be advice.

"We get your cousin Tisha to sign over guardianship." Sunni picked up her pen. "What's Tisha's number?"

"I—" Natalie managed a weak smile "—have no idea."

Lucky was back at Bernice's after spending the weekend on the road. He'd gone to Vinita, Oklahoma. He'd already paid the entry fee, and he needed the purse. Plus, he was going stir-crazy hanging around Bernice's place, waiting to hear from the lawyer and forcing himself not to drive to Natalie's place. Then, too, he was feeling guilty about keeping a secret from his mother. She was still in Selena, at the end of what she called a two-week vacation. She'd be heading back to Austin next weekend. He needed to tell her soon. He needed to call his father, too, but not until he was sure.

He could only call the last few days educational. He'd learned that when on the bull, he indeed *forgot* everything else, so great was his concentration. Off the bull, he *couldn't forget* Natalie and Robby Crosby. He remembered the way her hand automatically went to Robby's shoulders, a protective move. He remembered how her blue eyes snapped, looking right at him.

And he remembered Robby, who he could clearly see now looked so much like Marcus.

His body had been at the rodeo; his thoughts were in Selena, but Selena wasn't a paycheck. While Bernice served up breakfast, Lucky took out his calendar and started checking dates. At Vinita, he'd walked—okay, limped—away in third place. Respectable, yes. Advisable, no. He'd met up with Travis Needham there, and he and the rookie decided to travel together some. Made sense since Lucky's new jumping off place was Selena. Still, the commitment also reminded Lucky of his last partner, his brother.

Where was Lucky due next weekend? Could he afford to miss a rodeo or two and deal with Natalie and Robby, or did he need the standings? Before he had time to make a decision, his cell phone rang.

"Wish you wouldn't bring that to the table," his mother scolded, glowering at the phone.

He checked the number. Finally, his lawyer. He excused himself. Ten minutes later, he returned to the kitchen, having reached an agreement with his lawyer and had a disagreement with his father. Bernice busied herself by pouring more orange juice. Howie Junior stomped off to get ready for school.

"You know what I wish?" Lucky said.

"That you'd done better than third?" Bernice guessed.

He had to grin. Trust Bernice to cut to the chase. Too bad she had the wrong topic.

"That Bernice was making fried chicken again tonight." This guess came from his mother. They'd played the game before. Lots of times. Usually with Marcus. Never with their father. He'd found it a waste of time. "If you want to say something, say it," he'd demand. If they didn't manage to say the words in a certain amount of time, Henry Welch would put on his hat and be out the door.

Marcus tired of the game after a while, but Lucky never had.

"I wish things never changed."

His mother nodded, and Lucky knew she was thinking about Marcus, maybe even thinking of when her two boys had been young and dependent on her.

"Things have to change." Bernice handed Howie his lunch and ushered him to the porch just as the school bus pulled up out front.

Lucky looked out the window, at Howie running to the school bus. He and Marcus had walked to school or their mother had driven them. Big cities had the luxury of schools every few miles. Not so here in Selena. As a matter of fact, his mother had been bused to Selena from Delaney. She'd spent two hours a day on the bus.

"I never did homework," she'd joked. "I always did buswork."

When Bernice came back in the kitchen, Lucky pushed

aside his breakfast and asked, "Bern, do you have any pictures of us, me and Marcus, when we were little? Say about four or five."

"Ten, twelve or a hundred, probably."

"Can I see one when Marcus was, oh, about three or four?"

"Can you? Yes. May you? I don't know. Why?" She gave him a strange look and went to get a picture.

A moment later, Lucky studied the photo. She'd chosen one taken at his grandfather's place. He and Marcus stood in front of a carpet-covered barrel. Marcus wasn't looking at the camera. He concentrated on the practice barrel, and Lucky, who knew his older brother well, figured Marcus resented the time posing for the camera took away from the pretend bull. Lucky, ever the good son, looked right at the camera and grinned. Even at four, he was a poser.

"Mom, Bern, do you remember when we were this little?"

Bernice looked at Lucky's mom and took the picture. "Of course we remember when you were little. This was taken when you were about four. I think Marcus was five. Am I right, Betsy?"

Lucky's mom took the picture. A slow smile crossed her face. "Yes, I took the picture because every time my mother tried to get Marcus to stand still, he ran over and got on that barrel." Betsy chuckled. "Your grandmother got so mad she stomped into the house and said she didn't care if she ever got a picture of the two of you together or not. Somewhere, we have five or six pictures of Marcus standing on that barrel and you looking up at him."

Yes, Lucky looked up to his brother, even during Marcus's dark days.

Whoever loves his brother lives in the light, and there is nothing in time to make him stumble.

The Bible verse echoed in his heart as loneliness slammed into Lucky's gut with a force that almost uprooted him.

He missed Marcus. Oh, how he missed his brother.

"Mom, tomorrow I'm meeting with my lawyer."

His mother laid the picture on the table. "Why? Are you thinking that rodeo doctor could have done something more, that maybe Marcus needn't have died?"

"No," he said slowly, surprised that his mother jumped to such a conclusion so quickly. He almost lost his nerve.

"Lucas." Bernice used his given name. Not a good sign. "Why did you want me to fetch that picture? You want to tell us what's going on?"

"No, I don't want to tell you." He was still speaking too slowly, but he couldn't seem to help it. "But I probably need to."

And he needed for his father to be here, but per the three-minute phone call, Lucky knew that wouldn't be happening *yet*. Henry Stanton Welch's absence proved some things, some people, never changed. A few minutes ago, after he'd hung up from the lawyer, Lucky had called his father. He didn't mention Robby. Lucky only mentioned a family meeting, an *important* family meeting, and when could he come?

His father's first response was that the important family meeting should take place in Austin, and by his tone, Lucky knew that the word *important* didn't impress one bit. Next, Dad got out his calendar and couldn't decide. Finally, Lucky did what he usually did when trying to get through to his father. He gave up. Yet, in the long run, Lucky's father would be mad at missing this meeting. No, come to think of it, his father would be more than mad that he wasn't put in charge of the *problem*.

But Robby was not a problem; he was a gift. *Every good and perfect gift is from above, coming down from the Father of the heavenly lights, who does not change like shifting shadows.*

With that verse resonating in his mind, Lucky looked at the two women who'd stayed silent while he fought his memories. "I'm meeting with my lawyer tomorrow with and concerning Natalie Crosby."

He got out of his chair and came to kneel on the floor beside his mother. "Mom, by any chance did you see the little boy Natalie had with her at the rodeo?"

"No."

"Little Robby," Bernice supplied. "He's full of spit and vinegar. When he was a baby, his grandpa Leo would take him everywhere. Carried that baby seat like it was just another arm. I think he got three marriage proposals based on the way he loved that boy."

"That boy," Lucky said slowly, "is the spitting image of Marcus."

His mother's mouth opened, but no words came out.

Bernice's eyebrows drew together, then her lips pursed for just a moment before she said, "Oh. Oh. Oh…."

She might have "oh'd" forever except Lucky took the picture from his mother and walked it over to Bernice. "Tell me I'm wrong. You've seen Robby since he was little. Tell me I'm wrong."

"Oh, my." She looked up from the photo. "I can't quite grasp this. You think Robby is Marcus's son? No, little Natalie and Marcus? I just can't see…" Her words faded, but her facial expression didn't. She did see.

"Yes, little Natalie and Marcus," Lucky said. "Marcus has a son."

A chair screeched across the kitchen floor and Betsy, a wild look in her eyes, grabbed the photo from Bernice's hand. "Marcus? Marcus has a son? No way. We'd know."

Bernice's mouth was still open in a perfect 0. It looked like she wanted to say something. Silence didn't sit well with

Betsy. Lucky's mom grabbed Bernice by the arm. "Why do you look so spooked? This cannot be true."

"Oh, it just might be. What was I thinking? I remember seeing Natalie at the grocery store with Robby and thinking he was a good-looking kid. Why didn't I realize where he got his good looks from? Oh, my. What are you going to do, Lucky?"

Maybe change my stupid nickname, Lucky thought. He sure didn't feel lucky. He felt kicked in the stomach. All this time, his brother's son had been living in the same town as his mother's best friend, really only a stone's throw from where his mother grew up.

"And little Natalie Crosby's his mother," Aunt Bernice repeated. "She's a town favorite, you know."

He knew.

Not exactly a hanging offense.

Just an annoying roadblock.

"How old is he?" Mom asked.

"Three, he's three," Bernice said. "I remember when Natalie showed up with him. She went away to college and came home a mommy. Remember? I told you. And I couldn't imagine what kind of man wouldn't step up to the plate." She covered her mouth with her hand. The unspoken name "Marcus" lingering in the air.

"Robby. I have a grandson named Robby." Betsy sat back down, as pale as Lucky'd ever seen her.

"And I'm going to find out our rights tomorrow, when we meet with the lawyer."

Lucky's mother slumped forward, her eyes closed. Dark circles huddled under her eyes. "Three years, and nobody told us. We need to call your father and—"

"Mom, we're not sure about anything, the whys, the whats, the hows. That's why we're meeting tomorrow with lawyers. Let's tell Dad after we have proof, something tangible."

"Betsy, I'm still going to say that Natalie's a good girl. I'm—I'm flabbergasted at this information. I cannot picture her with Marcus…"

"Marcus never had trouble getting females," Betsy mumbled. "They started calling him when he was in second grade. His father and I, we tried to teach him right from wrong."

It was like Lucky wasn't there. Or worse, he was a teenager again. The irritable teenager who stood in his parents' living room while everyone discussed his future. Which college he would go to; what he would major in; whether he should live in the dorm the first few years or would an apartment be better?

Marcus had endured the same and had packed up in the middle of the night, left, and didn't call for two months.

Lucky'd disappointed them, too, but he'd been a man about it. He'd told his parents his plans.

Dad said not to let the door hit him on the way out.

This morning, Lucky's mother had the same look on her face as she'd had that night Lucky had walked out. Disappointment in life, disappointment in her children.

Why couldn't Lucky have found Robby in Timbuktu? Away from family, away from a family history that was so hurtful, where he'd have time to set things to right?

Probably because Timbuktu didn't have a rodeo.

Chapter Five

$\sim\!\!\mathfrak{G}$

Finding Tisha had become Natalie's number one—no, number two—duty. Robby came first. While Sunni searched the Internet for information on Tisha, Natalie used her dialing finger.

Neither venture garnered much progress. Sunni found three Tisha Crosbys, none the Tisha they were looking for. Natalie found the few postcards Tisha had sent. Since dropping off Robby, Tisha changed boyfriends and addresses about every six months, but judging by the postal marks, it had been over a year since she'd last made contact. Natalie really didn't have a single phone number. Using the return addresses and the Internet, in a week's time, Natalie found and spoke to a movie-star boyfriend, a dentist boyfriend and, of all things, an animal trainer. He'd sounded nice.

The most recent postcard proved to be the most difficult to track. According to Tisha's brief note, she was happy; he was wealthy. Natalie had an address and no name. At least on the earlier postcards there'd been names. It took Natalie three days to find a number. Judging by the clipped tones, Natalie figured Tisha hadn't made any friends in this household. According to the "Livingston Residence" Tisha'd been gone for two months, no forwarding address, and please don't call again.

At that point, Sunni made her next suggestion: hire a private detective to find Tisha.

Unfortunately, they'd only arrived at the decision yesterday. Today, Natalie and her lawyer had to meet with Lucky and his lawyer and hopefully delay any action.

Selena's courthouse was the oldest building in town. It was a redbrick monstrosity, a facade that misrepresented the town's size and importance. Natalie stepped from her car and pulled her coat tighter around her. Texas weather, ever fickle, had changed from warm to cold in the blink of an eye.

The chill seemed foreboding. The sting of the weather matched the biting fear that gripped her heart.

She saw her lawyer's car, but, unfortunately, she didn't see Sunni.

Robby was over at Patty's, enjoying a day on the farm and getting dirty. Patty would feed him candy and let him follow her own kids around. He'd eat dirt and have a wonderful time.

"Are you all right?"

Natalie blinked. She'd been standing beside her car, not moving. And, wouldn't you know it, Lucky Welch was now standing next to her.

"No, I'm not."

"I'm not, either," he said gently.

He didn't look like a bull rider today. He looked like an urban professional. He wore light brown slacks and a white dress shirt. Over it, he had a too-small brown jacket. One that emphasized the broadness of his shoulders, the strength in his arms. He still wore boots, well-worn and also brown.

"Can we just stop this?" Natalie asked hopefully. "Turn around and pretend I never approached you?"

"No," he said. "My mother's waiting at Bernice's. It was all I could do to keep her from attending. We need to come to some solutions today that work for both of us because I have to let my father know all that's going on, and the more we decide together, you and I, the easier it will be."

"This day is not going to be easy," Natalie predicted.

"It's going to be a lot easier than if my father was involved. If he were involved, you'd need a more expensive lawyer, and I wouldn't be using a man I love and trust who specializes in sports law."

Sports law? Lucky Welch was using a man he loved and trusted and not a cutthroat? Natalie studied Lucky's face. He looked sad, lonely, and maybe even wistful.

She wished she looked the same. She looked, felt, terrified, lonely and threatened. Not the combination she really wanted. But one she deserved. A moment's desperation, a rash act, had culminated in this.

She turned and walked away. Lucky Welch, the preacher, may have been sincere when he asked, *"Are you all right?"* But he was also sincere when he said, *"You're going to need a more expensive lawyer."*

He was not on her side.

They met in a conference room. It was as brown as Lucky's outfit and smelled like Lysol. Lucky's lawyer, Paul Wilfong, didn't act expensive. Lucky was dressed better than Mr. Wilfong. The lawyer wore jeans, a flannel shirt and boots that looked like they needed to be replaced.

Sunni nodded for Natalie to take a seat on one side of the table. She put a slim folder on the surface and sat beside Natalie. Before she could protest, Paul Wilfong was helping adjust her chair.

Sunni's lips pressed together.

Wilfong just grinned.

If this were any other place or time, Natalie might enjoy the show, but if this Wilfong fellow was putting on a show, it had better not be to disarm them.

"Let's begin," Sunni said after both Lucky and Wilfong sat down.

Wilfong looked at Natalie and remarked, "You sure do resemble Tisha."

Natalie felt Sunni's hand gently pat her knee. Good thing, because Natalie didn't have the breath to respond. Sunni said, "We're here to talk about the custody of Robert Crosby."

"No middle name?" Lucky said, seemingly to nobody.

"No."

Wilfong, apparently, didn't have a folder to place on the table. He also didn't carry a briefcase. He folded his hands in front of him. "Let's pray first."

Without argument, Sunni and Lucky both bowed their heads. Natalie sat stunned. Bowing her head seemed almost to imply an agreement, and she didn't want to agree to anything. And since when did a meeting requiring legal assistance start with a prayer?

Her father's lawyer never prayed.

After his "amen," Mr. Wilfong looked at both women. Then he said in a voice that sent a chill down Natalie's spine, "I'm not a children's advocate. I've never handled a custody case. I do, however, know the right lawyer to steer Lucky to, and I also know, having children myself, that if you two can come to an agreement outside the courtroom, it's best for everyone. Madam, do you have something to say?"

Natalie glanced at Sunni. Sunni had been hoping to speak first. The prayer certainly one-upped that idea. Sunni had wanted to set the stage, the tone, and have the upper hand because, truthfully, the team of Natalie and Sunni had only one weapon to support their claim to Robby: the guardianship papers Tisha had yet to sign.

Sunni was looking at Lucky. Her hand was atop the folder. Inside that folder lay the birth certificate, a paper that would end the negotiations right now and Lucky wouldn't need a high-dollar lawyer.

"I say," Sunni said easily, "we leave the room and let these two see what they can come up with without us."

"I'd like that," Lucky said. If trustworthy was searching for a national spokesperson, then judging by the look on Lucky's face, the self-assured way he held himself, he'd be the man for the job.

"Natalie, say the words. Tell me to go or to stay. You're in charge," Sunni prodded.

Great, just great. If Natalie said no, she'd be the one dragging her feet, the one not willing to be a team player. If she said yes, she alone would be negotiating Robby's future. She swallowed and said, "I'll stay. You go."

Wilfong opened the door for Sunni. On the way out, her lawyer's eyes fell on the folder still lying on the table. Then, her eyes raised to meet Natalie's. One tiny nod encouraged Natalie that she could do it.

When the door closed, Natalie noticed that she and Lucky sat in a room without a window. She pressed her lips together. Trapped. In a hole she'd dug herself.

"You want to take a walk?" Lucky suggested. "We don't have to stay here." Suddenly, he appeared chagrined. "I mean, it doesn't hurt you to walk, does it?"

"What? I can walk." For a moment, Natalie was confused. "Oh, someone told you about the accident. My leg only hurts, really, when the weather is about to change or I'm really stressed."

Lucky grinned. "I'll take the fact that it doesn't hurt as a good sign. You're not stressed."

"Yet," Natalie said. "Or maybe I've been so stressed lately that my body no longer recognizes stress."

"I'm going to stand by my original thought, that you're not stressed." Lucky stood and came around the table. "Let's walk. I know it's cold, but there's a diner just down the street. I'd love some coffee, and we'll be in—" he looked around "—a little less sterile environment."

"Okay." Natalie stood and took the folder. It lay accusingly on the table, a constant reminder of how impossible it was to discern right from wrong *emotionally*. Folding it, she put it in her purse and prayed she wouldn't need to open it.

Lucky walked slow enough. While Natalie waved at people she knew, people who would be sure to call later and ask about the young man she was with, he rambled about the weather, about his mother, about Delaney and about his love for small towns.

Right. Sure.

Like some rodeo Romeo would be willing to settle for one choice at the movie theater, no McDonald's and streets that rolled up at nine unless you were a drinker.

Okay, his grandparents were from practically next door in Delaney, and it wasn't fair for her to compare Lucky to Marcus.

Right before the waitress seated them in a back booth, Lucky mentioned seeing her father's grave.

"When did you see it?" she asked.

"Last week. I headed for Delaney. I wanted to drive by my grandparents' place. Then I stopped at the cemetery."

"Makes sense. I probably should have realized. How many years has your family been in the area?" She was surprised to discover she really wanted to know. Lucky, either by the gift of gab or by a burning desire to make her like him, had managed to find topics that felt safe.

"My grandpa moved to Delaney in 1942, following his parents. They were in Abilene first. I think we've had family in West Texas for at least a hundred years."

"You'd love my living room," Natalie said. "Dad put up pictures from when the ranch was just starting. We have pictures of the Selena and Delaney area dating back more than a hundred years. My favorite old tintype shows what looks to me like an outhouse but I think is actually the original house."

"I'd love to see it," Lucky said.

Suddenly, the menu looked like a good defense. Natalie picked hers up and held it so it covered her face. What had she just done? Invited him over? No, no, no. Maybe the gift of gab was beneficial only to the speaker. She'd just walked into a trap.

When she put the menu down, not even noticing a single item she hungered for, Lucky was studying her.

"Natalie, I can't even imagine how uncomfortable you are, how threatened you feel, but, believe me, I, my family, we don't want to be the enemy. We want to help. We want to get to know Marcus's little boy, and if we can make this a win-win situation, everybody, especially Robby, benefits. Please meet me halfway."

The waitress came at that moment. Lucky ordered coffee and a cinnamon roll. Natalie decided on iced tea. When it arrived, she took a long drink and then said, "What do you want?"

He took a folded piece of paper from his pocket and stared at it. "Paul has a typed, more legalized version of this, but my notes are the same." Looking at her, he said, "My mother and I put this together yesterday." He slid the paper across the table. "Here."

He wrote in all capital letters. They were straight, and he seemed to like leaving extra spaces between each word. The top half of the paper was labeled "short-term." The bottom half was labeled "long-term." Each half had only three items.

Six altogether.

Six too many.

Short-term, he wanted Robby to be introduced to the Welches, first as friends, then as family. He wanted that to happen sometime next week. As if he knew right where she was reading, he said, "You can tell him on your own, or we could maybe have a cookout at Bernice's. Neutral territory. She loves you and says she can't imagine a better single parent. But you don't need to be a single parent. We'll help. Bernice said you dropped out of college to raise Robby. If you want to go back, we'll help with money."

"What?" She glanced at the paper, and then back up at him. Going back to school, for her, was listed under long-term, along with money negotiations and holidays.

"We'll help with money...."

"Are you for real?"

He pinched himself, exaggerating, and with a grin on his face. It looked silly, but it did take an edge off the fear that was starting to pool in her stomach again.

"I'm for real."

"This is happening so fast. I mean, I've hired Sunni Foreman just to try to make sense of what legal rights—" she almost said *I have.* Instead, she said, "—you have. She seems to think quite a bit. My dad says—said—not to completely trust lawyers. I'm pretty sure he'd also be inclined not to trust you."

"Your dad must have been quite a man. I hear he looked after Robby as his own. I'm only sorry that I can't shake his hand, thank him, on behalf of our family."

He reached across the table and put his hand over hers. She almost tugged it away, almost made a face, but again, he looked so sincere.

"I'm gone most weekends to rodeos, and people are counting on me. But I'm going to take to flying a bit more now and also make Selena my home base."

Well, that would take care of the next two items on the short-term list. After the initial meeting, Lucky wanted to take Robby to church on Wednesday evenings, and then he wanted the family to have permission to visit at least one Saturday a month.

Lucky continued, "I'm making Robby my business, at least until we're all comfortable with where we fit in as a family. Please agree to the potluck at Bernice's. I promise, we'll take everything slow. First, this Saturday, and then we'll wait a few weeks before we either do church or a family outing. If it seems too fast for Robby, we can wait a little while before we tell him. But he needs to know us. We want to know him. We're going to make sure my brother Marcus's son has everything he needs. And, as Robby's mother, we'd like the same for you."

Natalie swallowed. The words sounded so innocent. And they were true. She'd dropped out of school to take care of Robby. Robby, who *was* Marcus's son, *not* Natalie's.

The son Marcus apparently hadn't known about.

"If I say yes to this meeting, to letting your family get to know Robby, all you want to do is help, be involved, not take?" Her voice broke. Just three weeks ago, she'd lost her father. He'd been taken from her. Today, sitting across from her, was the man who could easily take Robby away.

"All you want to do is help, get to know Robby," she repeated slowly.

"Yes."

The folder remained in her purse. She didn't need it. For a moment, she was safe. The list went with it. Lucky wanted to get to know Robby, take the boy to church, help financially and, so far, *without legal strings*. If she agreed, then the birth certificate remained hidden, at least for now.

"Okay," Natalie said. "We'll come to the potluck. Depending on how that day goes, I'll tell him you're related to his father."

She half expected him to whoop; instead, he bent his head. His lips moved, and she could hear his muffled words of thanks.

Lucky was thanking God for answering his prayer. Only Natalie knew that Lucky's prayer was misdirected and that he deserved a lot more than he was receiving.

The phone call came early morning Wednesday while Natalie uploaded, cropped and then enhanced jewelry photos for one of her clients. The finishing touches, and the ones that kept her clients with her, were the details. For this client, she added what she called diamond dazzle. When a prospective buyer went to the Web site, not only would the display be attractive, but the jewelry the client most wanted sold would sparkle, literally.

Playing with dazzle wasn't enough to keep Natalie from worrying.

All Tuesday afternoon and evening, she'd been expecting the ax to fall, expecting to find that the list that looked so simple was not. So hearing Betsy Welch's voice on the other end of the phone was no surprise.

After all, Natalie and Lucky had met just yesterday, sent their lawyers home and agreed on the short-term. But there were twenty-four hours between yesterday and today. Hours that were probably a long time to a grandmother who wanted to meet her only grandson.

Betsy Welch managed to turn Natalie's name into Nat-tal-lee. Natalie's own grandmother had done the same, and Mrs. Welch wept more than she spoke. Maybe the tears were more responsible for the name mangling than the Texas drawl.

Natalie left the computer. Mood always affected her over-all performance. Her client wouldn't want to see a digital smorgasbord of black, brooding diamonds when it came to his display. Instead of pounding on the computer keys, Natalie paced in front of the couch as Lucky's mother talked about wanting to get to know Robby, and about her son Marcus—she assumed, of course, Natalie really knew him—and about staying in Selena longer. Natalie winced at that pronounce-ment and kicked a toy train out of the way before bending down to pick up a pillow. One thing for sure, if this woman was wrangling for an invitation to the house, she wasn't getting one. Right now Natalie's living room did not look like something from the pages of *Better Homes and Gardens*. It looked like *Return of the Three-Year-Old Tornado*.

But Mrs. Welch didn't ask if she could stop by the house, pretend to be selling household goods or a church lady. Betsy wanted something else, something a little more convenient, something straight from the list, except that it was an item Lucky and Natalie had agreed to put on hold. "Let's meet at church tonight. Real innocent. Just let me see him. I need to see him. I—"

When Betsy finally took a breath, Natalie jumped in. "I'll think about it." A no-frills answer, and one that shut Mrs. Welch up, until Robby ran into the room, that is.

"Momma, who's on the phone? Why I no get to answer?"

"You were asleep, honey."

He nodded, an exaggerated response and reached for the phone. Until Pop Pop's death, they'd been letting Robby pick up the beloved instrument and say "Hi" before taking the phone and giving a real salutation.

To Robby, getting to answer or at least talk on the phone was as good as Christmas.

"It's a lady I know. She's inviting us to church tonight."

"Church?"

"Yes, you know, where Patty and Daniel go every Wednesday and Sunday?"

"Oh, yeah. We go?"

"We're not sure." Natalie looked at the phone. Betsy Welch was still talking. Natalie could hear her asking, "Is that Robby?"

Maybe Natalie should call Sunni Foreman. Lucky had walked her to Sunni's office after she'd agreed to a Saturday outing at Bernice's and after they'd finished eating. It had been a long walk, all of fifteen minutes, and all Natalie could think of was that Lucky Welch was making this his home base just to be near his nephew.

Right. How long would it last?

He was rodeo from his hat to his heart, and he was in his prime.

It wouldn't last.

But Lucky wasn't Marcus.

And what really bothered Natalie was that after she repeated, "We'll think about it," and hung up, her first impulse was to call Lucky.

After all, it was his list she'd agreed to; it was his list she'd stared at last night when sleep refused to visit. Yes, church attendance was on it. But they'd agreed to start slowly, with Saturday.

One day after their initial meeting was definitely not slowly. One day after their initial meeting, and things were already changing, meant Natalie had to tell Robby a few things about family, and pray that her family—namely Tisha—stayed away until Natalie could sort out what to do, what to say, *how long she could hide,* and the guardianship issue.

Mrs. Welch suggested an innocent meeting tonight. An "Oh, by the way, Robby, these are some people you need to know" kind of thing. And Natalie, already skittish, felt threatened.

By church as much as by Betsy Welch.

Natalie had gone to church with Patty when they were kids. Vacation Bible School was fun, lots of Kool-Aid and animal crackers, but other than that, it was a lot of sitting still and being quiet. It would drive Robby nuts. He wasn't a sit-still kind of child. What if he misbehaved? What if Betsy Welch determined Natalie wasn't a good mother?

Natalie hadn't agreed to attend, but she hadn't disagreed, either. It wasn't easy to say no to a crying grandmother. Her father would say she was prolonging the inevitable. Well, so be it. Then again, her lawyer would say she was tempting fate.

Her lawyer attended the Main Street Church. Yesterday afternoon, with Lucky's visitation wishes spread on the lawyer's desk, Sunni asked, "If the roles were reversed, and Robby was your kin and being raised by someone else, is this list more than, just right or less than what you would hope for?"

The list was less than she'd have asked for. Anyone who knew Robby, the kind of kid he was, the joy he brought, would know that no list of sporadic meetings here and there would be enough.

"It's a reasonable request," Natalie had agreed.

Just her luck to find a lawyer who reasoned and who valued right over money.

There'd be no Monday-night movie made about Sunni. What you saw was what you got.

Almost too perfect.

And right there in the office, Natalie had seen a picture of Sunni Foreman standing with a group of kids all wearing Main Street Church Bible Bowl Champions 2008 shirts.

"I wanna go to church. Let's go." Robby was up for anything and truly believed that the next place was better than the place he was. It was a characteristic he'd inherited from Tisha.

That comparison was so truly right-on, Natalie sank onto the couch and whispered, "Oh, no."

"What wrong, Mommy?"

"Nothing. Just something Mommy needs to do. Go get your trains while I make a few phone calls. When I'm done, I'll build a track with you."

Robby's eyes lit up. His favorite thing! Next to talking on the phone and going somewhere and Christmas. They were going to put train tracks together. Life just didn't get any better.

Oh, to be three again.

"We play train!" he jabbered excitedly.

"In just a minute." That's all it took. A moment later, Robby dug out his blue track and was sorting his trains by which had working batteries and which needed new ones.

Most of the trains needed batteries. Batteries had been Pop Pop's job. Natalie knew where they were, how to put them in, but she cried every time.

Batteries were Pop Pop's job.

Bandages were Natalie's job, but they didn't make one big enough to fix all that was wrong in their lives at the moment.

Chapter Six

The Main Street Church put every other building in Selena to shame. It received a fresh coat of white paint every year, and if Natalie didn't know better, she'd suspect the minister, Tate Brown, even spray painted the lawn green.

Natalie, following the Selena church crowd's example, pulled into the parking lot at the exact moment church began. Just two spots down, Patty was unloading her kids.

"Girl!" she called. "I can't keep up with you. You about knocked me down when you called. First the rodeo, now church. Are you sure you know what you're doing?"

"No, I'm not sure." And she wasn't, but Sunni thought church more a neutral ground than Bernice's house. Grandma Welch would have to curb her enthusiasm in front of a crowd of virtual strangers. Natalie would be the only stranger, really, at Bernice's house on Saturday.

After getting the go-ahead from Sunni, Natalie phoned Patty to make sure she would be at church that evening. No way did Natalie want to go without a friend by her side during the evening service.

Since her father's death, she'd felt so alone. Surprisingly, just being in the church parking lot diminished some of those feelings. The place felt alive as friends shouted back and forth, parents hurried bundled children toward the doors and her best friend from childhood opened her arms for a hug.

Robby hit the ground and headed toward Patty. He knew a good hug when he saw one. He hopped the whole way. "We go church!" he announced, not only to Patty but also to the couple parking their car next to hers, and to the elderly man who wisely stopped walking to let the three-year-old careen by.

Natalie shook her head. "How about I pack Robby up tomorrow and we come out to the farm for a whole day?"

"Perfect," Patty said, bending down and lifting Robby up. "We'll come up with a battle plan just in case you need warriors, I mean, friends."

Daniel let go of Patty's husband's hand and ran around to take Robby's. Without so much as a by-your-leave, they disappeared up the steps and into the church. Patty rescued her nine-month-old from the car seat before turning to Natalie.

"And, as concerned as I am about what's going on between you and the Welches, it's still good to see you here at church."

Natalie looked at the white clapboard building and suddenly realized it hadn't been all that long since she'd passed through the front door.

Her father's funeral.

Before her feet could slow or her mouth protest, the minister opened the door and stepped out. The sound of singing spilled out of the auditorium. Still, as if he didn't care that he wasn't where he was supposed to be, his greeting was as enthusiastic as Patty's.

"Natalie Crosby! An answer to my prayers…well, one of them at least. Good to have you here. Patty, are you responsible for her attendance today?"

"Only if you count my prayers as responsible."

"Nat-tal-lee." The third greeting came from Betsy Welch. She'd followed the minister and now stood at the top of the steps looking down. Her hair was the same color as Robby's. And tall…this woman and her hair were tall. Nevertheless, Betsy had on cowboy boots with a more-than-decent heel. On a good day, Natalie might have headed up the steps and tried for an even match. On a good day, she'd reach Betsy Welch's shoulder.

But it wasn't a good day.

"Where's Robby?" Betsy asked.

"He already went inside with my son," Patty said. She gave Natalie a side look and went up the stairs. "I'm Patty Dunbar. You must be Mrs. Welch?"

Betsy nodded.

"We all love Natalie," Patty said, emphasizing every word. "She's a great mother."

"That she is." Lucky stepped up beside his mother. "Robby looks happy and healthy and—"

"I understand he looks like a Welch." Betsy murmured the words, but to Natalie, they might as well have shouted.

If Natalie read the minister's facial expression correctly, then the minister was quickly realizing that the group on the steps were not strangers, and that his job as a preacher just might be needed.

"Ma'am." He turned to Betsy, no doubt figuring she was the catalyst, along with Natalie. "Is there—"

"Mommy—" Robby appeared in the doorway "—you coming?"

"Oh, my." Betsy's hands fluttered to her chest.

Robby suddenly realized he was the center of attention and grinned. He took two steps toward Natalie and halted. Looking back up, he studied Betsy Welch. Then, before

Natalie could move or say a thing, he bounded back up the stairs and held out his arms.

Betsy Welch was more than willing to bend down, pick him up and hold him *like she'd never let go*.

Lucky felt sorry for the preacher. The man didn't know who to go to first. Lucky took one step, heading down the stairs, thinking Natalie might need someone to lean on.

Looks were deceiving. Natalie, with only the barest trace of a limp, advanced up the stairs.

"Mom," Lucky said, standing still, somewhat of a block between Natalie and his mother. "This is Robby Crosby, the boy I was telling you about. He came to the rodeo Saturday. He's quite the little cowboy."

"Yes, I can see he is." Betsy stroked Robby's hair and jiggled him up and down, causing giggles and making the little boy hold her even tighter.

"I not little," Robby protested. "I big."

"I can see that, too," Betsy cooed.

The door to the church opened again, and the preacher's wife poked her head out. "Tate, we've gone through three songs, and the congregation is wondering where you are."

Tate obediently looked at his watch, then looked at the group on the steps and said, "We'd better go in."

Natalie had already reached the top of the stairs. Lucky's mother didn't even notice. Natalie held out her arms, and Robby obediently turned toward her but didn't acknowledge her arms. He shook his head. "No."

This time Lucky managed to be in the right place. He put one hand on Natalie's back and the other nudged his mother forward.

"Mom," he said gently. "It's time to go in."

His mother blinked, noticed Natalie and held on to Robby.

"Mommy." Robby was blissfully unaware of the tension. "There's choo-choo in the classroom. Can I have a gink?"

"Of course you can have a drink," Natalie said. "And remember, when we go in the doors you need to talk in your quiet, inside voice."

Lucky held open the door, glad the preacher was in a hurry and glad that his mother had been in the preacher's way so that she had to enter before everyone else.

"Sorry," he whispered in Natalie's ear. "She called you while I was outside showing Howie Junior what to do with his free hand when he's riding. I about fell over when she told me what she'd done."

"I about fell over when she called," Natalie admitted.

"I really appreciate your coming tonight. It's the first time since Marcus's death that she's been this happy. She practically danced as we were heading to the car for church."

Natalie didn't respond. She clutched her purse and hurried after his mother. It was almost comical. His mother practically floated, she was so happy. What Natalie, a good foot shorter, was doing could only be described as a march, a very determined march.

Gumption, she had gumption. If she were Marcus's rebound from Tisha, then Marcus was blind. This woman shouldn't be anybody's rebound.

That thought led to another. Maybe it hadn't been rebound. Maybe there'd actually been a courtship. The people in town knew nothing about it, but Natalie had spent two years in college, away from the prying eyes of the community.

Had she loved Marcus?

Oh, he hoped so. His brother deserved at least that. Of course, if she loved Marcus, *why didn't she contact the family after Marcus died?* Let them know then that Robby existed and needed family.

Did she need comfort? Of course she did. Especially now. She'd just lost her own father and so soon after Marcus's death. No wonder she was tense.

Since Marcus's death, Lucky had more than once sermonized how the Father's comfort had been his only comfort.

He had always wondered how the nonchurched had the strength to put one step in front of the other when sorrow struck. God was Lucky's strength.

"Praise be the God and Father of our Lord Jesus Christ, the Father of compassion and the God of all comfort, who comforts us in all our troubles, so that we can comfort those in any trouble with the comfort we ourselves have received from God."

"What?" Natalie turned to face him. She'd caught up to his mother, and now Robby was more than ready to return to Natalie. Her hand was solidly against Robby's back, and the boy had placed his cheek right next to Natalie's and was grinning ear to ear.

"I didn't mean to say the verse out loud," Lucky said. Still, he admitted to himself, it was probably good that he had.

According to Bernice, Natalie didn't attend church and neither had her father. Robby was not being raised to know God. Lucky'd mentioned church as a long-term goal, and Natalie hadn't objected, but now he could see Natalie needed a church home, too.

"That was a verse from the Bible?" She sounded incredulous.

"Yes."

Her words softened, and he was gladdened by the look in her eyes.

"That's right," she said. "You're a preacher, too. No wonder you're glad Robby's here."

He could have corrected her, but he didn't.

He wasn't glad Robby was there. He was glad Robby *and Natalie* were there.

Wednesday-night services were a whole lot different from the Sunday mornings Natalie dimly remembered. Instead of going to an exciting Bible class and then sitting in the auditorium for a whole hour, they sat in the auditorium—Robby nestled between Natalie and Mrs. Welch—while songs were led, announcements read and a prayer offered. Five minutes in, Robby wriggled from his seat, got permission from Natalie and went to sit by Daniel.

Natalie forced herself to relax. Robby was mesmerized by a new place full of potential playmates and, in his opinion, full of noise. If all these people could sing at the top of their lungs, why couldn't he shout? He said "MOM" in a loud voice during lulls at least four times—each time with a bit more volume. She and Mrs. Welch both leaned forward and said "Shh!" When the congregation looked, most nudged each other and Natalie could just imagine their whispers. *"Is that the Crosby girl? Who's she with?"*

About the time she was ready to head for the foyer, Robby's hand firmly tucked in hers and the "inside voice" lecture at the ready, a voice from the podium boomed, "You are dismissed," and almost everyone stood. Robby, no dummy, used the opportunity to edge away.

Fifteen minutes had passed in a blink. "What are we doing?" Natalie whispered to Patty as they followed the masses into the foyer and down the hall, keeping the kids in sight.

"It's time for class. Robby's already found his."

Ah, yes, the choo-choo classroom.

Patty stayed by Natalie's side as they headed down a

hallway and followed Robby into a room decorated with a pint-
size table, a puppet box and lots of toy boxes. Five small
children were already there. Two sat at a table putting together
puzzles. One ran around the room, holding a paper plate and
chanting, *"The wheels on da bus. The wheels on da bus."*
Robby and another child had their heads buried in one of the
toy chests. Five little trains were soon scattered across the
floor.

"Good, we have a visitor tonight." The teacher—surprise,
surprise—a man, boomed as he entered the room. Immediately, all save Robby headed for him, bashed right into his
knees, and they all tumbled to the ground in laughter.

Robby put down a train, and after just a moment's contem-
plation, joined right in.

Nope, this was not the church service Natalie remembered.

Patty tugged at Natalie's arm, dragging her from the classroom and out into the hall again. "He'll be fine. Mr. Chris is
an excellent teacher. I almost wish Daniel was still in his
class."

"Where are we going?" Natalie asked as they moved down
the hall again.

"Right now there are three adult classes offered. One is
called 'Discipleship.' Um, probably not for you, *yet*. One is
for young parents. I'm going to that one. The last is about
Paul."

"Paul who?"

"Wow," Patty said. "I don't think I've ever been asked that
question. Let's go to the young parents' class. I'll tell you later
about Paul, but I'm going to need a lot more time."

"And what she can't tell you, I can," Lucky Welch whispered in her ear.

Only he wasn't whispering in her ear, he was simply
standing behind her. For some reason, he felt so close, she

could feel the words against her cheek like a caress; each word was warm, heated and deep, like the man who spoke them. One look over her shoulder and Natalie knew Lucky had no idea of his effect on her.

Better to keep it that way.

Against her will, she shivered as they entered a classroom already filled with about thirty people who were all chattering comfortably. They weren't all young, either. Natalie recognized the Pruitts, who were now raising grandchildren. Allison sat in the back of the room, a notebook in hand, looking exhausted. Natalie probably should join her and complete the single-mother corner. For the first time in a long time, she considered Allison her friend. If things had been different, if Tisha hadn't been in the picture, then Allison and Natalie would still be the best of friends, sharing Mommy stories, and swapping babysitting. But Natalie was too afraid of what Allison knew.

The rest of the classroom was occupied by young couples, mothers *and fathers*.

"My mother went to the class on Discipleship," Lucky whispered as they all sat down.

"Good," Natalie whispered back.

Patty's husband welcomed everyone and then started a video. Natalie relaxed. She wouldn't need to talk, share or even act interested. She was a master at zoning out when the television was on. Two full years of cartoons had perfected the art.

The segment on raising children, this night, focused on birth order. Natalie didn't close her eyes all the way. Maybe this would be interesting. She'd been an only child. The doctors didn't know why her parents couldn't have more, but she hadn't heard them complain.

During her adolescence, she'd complained, loud and clear. Onlys, especially those who lived a distance from town, didn't often have playmates. Onlys never won an argument because the only people around to argue with were parents. According to the program, onlys needed to be exposed to other children, playgroups and such. Natalie agreed. A few years ago, her dad finally admitted that keeping her from being a lonely "only" was why they'd had her cousin Tisha out so often.

Natalie figured Tisha's parents were partly responsible, too. With eight children to feed, having one out of the way might be a relief. Dad's younger brother was dirt-poor and when money came their way, it left just as quickly. The words *gambling problem* were bantered around. What Natalie remembered most about Tisha's visits was how Tisha thought Natalie's closet was her closet, and how Tisha seemed to know just where and what Natalie was doing and managed to get there first.

If this birth-order film was to be believed, Tisha did indeed have "oldest child syndrome." She believed she was superior and knew everything.

"I'm the baby," Lucky whispered.

Instead of responding, Natalie closed her eyes and tried to clear her head. Lately, Tisha'd been on her mind way too much, thanks to Natalie's own misstep inviting the Welches into their lives.

Lucky was supposed to give her money and then disappear, like Marcus had done with Tisha, not stick around and offer support, support and more support.

"Are you really a baby?" she finally whispered back.

"I think if I believe this guy, I'm more of a middle. I'm certainly not a prankster, but I am a salesman and an entrepreneur."

"Salesman?" Natalie questioned.

"I think all preachers are salesmen with a winning product."

"That's a funny way to think of it," Patty said doubtfully.

Someone coughed about then, and Natalie became uncomfortably aware that quite a few people were watching them instead of the television scene.

So, birth order wasn't a given. Now in Dad's family, he had been the oldest and fit the stereotype. He'd been responsible and a leader. His much-younger brother, Allen, Tisha's dad, had been a prankster. He'd been kicked out of high school, didn't try college and settled for working for his wife's family at their dairy. They were dirt-poor, but that's not why Tisha didn't try to leave Robby with them. Even Tisha, as jaded as she was, knew that it didn't just take money to raise a happy and healthy child. Tisha's parents were also the most unhappy people in the state. Bad luck, bad choices and hard work had taken a toll on Allen and his wife.

He'd been left half of what was now Natalie's ranch, but sold it to Natalie's dad before she, or any of his children, were born. Her dad always felt somewhat guilty about it because while Allen had been paid good money, the value had skyrocketed a decade later, and he could have had so much more.

They'd come to hear the reading of the will. Robby had thought it great fun to have five second cousins, once removed, in the house. It didn't phase him that they spent their time either in front of the television or playing video games.

What Natalie remembered most was how Tisha's parents weren't surprised to find that the money was gone.

Allen no longer had a gambling problem; he now had an I've-given-up-on-life problem.

Natalie's dad had left them money. Since, at the time, there appeared to be no money, they'd left without it. Now, Natalie considered, she could make good on her dad's intention. She could send them the money. She'd address the envelope and check to Allen's wife.

"It's time to pray." Patty's husband was standing up again, and the video no longer provided insights into birth order. Looking over at Lucky, Natalie watched as he finished penciling a note into the margin of his already well-scribbled-in Bible and bowed his head. He looked peaceful. In the back of the room, Allison closed her notebook. She no longer looked exhausted. She looked serene, even happy.

On Natalie's other side, Patty was smiling, but Patty smiled most of the time. Before bowing her head, Patty reached over and took Natalie's hand. Up in front of the room, Patty's husband prayed about the coming Thanksgiving holiday, about the sick and about the lost. Everyone else looked content.

Natalie had never felt so lost.

Lucky's mother chatted happily as they pulled away from the Main Street Church. Her bright red nails beat a frantic tap, tap, tap against the door handle. She was as excited as he'd ever seen her, and his mother excited easily.

Nothing compared to this evening.

She wanted to buy Robby a pony. She wanted to decorate a room for him at her house. She wanted to buy a second home here in Selena so she could be easily accessible should she be needed. She wanted so much Lucky almost felt out of breath just keeping up with her.

He wanted a few things, too.

He wanted not to be around when his mother fell back down to Earth. No way would Robby be getting a pony anytime soon. The empty barn was a testimony to Natalie's fear. His mother decorating a room was fine, but Lucky didn't want to be around when she mentioned the idea to his father. As for buying a second home, Lucky figured that argument would be won or lost about the time his mother mentioned decorating a bedroom for what his father would consider a "surprise" grandson.

His mother was having trouble staying true to the short-term, and boy could she dream about the long-term. Lucky was more a realist. More than anything, he wanted Natalie to realize she wasn't losing Robby but gaining family.

No, more than anything, Lucky wanted his father to be open to the idea of Robby, wholeheartedly accept him and support everyone involved.

If the prodigal son had had a son, he'd have been welcomed in his father's home.

Lucky's father didn't welcome any son who went against his wishes. Ever.

"Mom, what have *you* told Dad?"

The tapping fingers stilled. "After you came home from the meeting yesterday, I decided to call Henry. It's not fair to keep this from him. I told him there was something I needed to tell him, but he sounded busy so I didn't tell him what." She stared out the window instead of at Lucky. He didn't blame her. Her whole life she'd learned to approach her husband from the side and never straight-on.

Well, maybe not her whole life. He and Marcus had found pictures from when their parents dated. There'd been a time when their father smiled, laughed and spent time with family.

That part of his dad no longer existed by the time Lucky came along. Maybe if it did, his mother wouldn't be angst-ridden and maybe Marcus wouldn't be—

No, don't go there.

His mother took a deep breath and finally looked at him. "You didn't tell him, either." Her words were somewhat accusatory.

Sometimes Lucky wondered how his mother kept her sanity. He and Marcus left at age eighteen. His mother stayed, and this year she'd be celebrating twenty-eight years of staying.

"I'm going to call him tonight."

The evening shadows made the town an eerie gray and black. A wind sent the trees shivering. His mother shivered, too. "We have to," Lucky said, "and the sooner the better. We probably should have told him before we negotiated our visitation requests."

"What do you think he'll do?" Mom asked.

For the first time in years, Lucky truly didn't have an answer. His father was fast approaching sixty and Lucky couldn't remember the man ever having fun, ever being open to new ideas. There were rodeo clowns past sixty who knew how to embrace life. How to have fun. Some of them worked harder than Lucky; some of them played harder than Lucky. They epitomized fun, and most of them initiated new ideas. Never, not in Lucky's memory, had Henry Welch given permission for anyone—not himself, not his children—to take a risk, make a poor choice or live down a mistake.

The father Lucky knew would demand paternity tests, consider Robby an embarrassment, and then he'd still turn his back on Marcus's son.

The way he'd turned his back on Marcus.

Risks, poor choices and mistakes had no place in Lucky's dad's life.

"What do you think he'll do?" Lucky's mother repeated softly.

"I'm not sure, Mom, but it doesn't matter. Robby is what matters."

She nodded and went back to staring out the window. Her bubbly mood was gone.

Bernice had beaten them home. No surprise since Lucky's

mother had to escort her grandson to the car, had to say "Bye" fifteen times and had to contain herself and her words because the little boy didn't know the woman cooing over him was his grandma.

The porch light was on. Lucky's mother went up the stairs and into the house without a word. Lucky followed slowly, nodding a greeting to Bernice's family and then heading upstairs. Mary's room didn't look inviting, and the grays and blacks outdoors deepened. It was nine at night. His dad would be in his office, books open, not even remembering that for the rest of his family, it was church night.

Lucky went straight to the table by the window and set his Bible down. He didn't need to open it. The scriptures he needed swirled in his mind like bumper cars connecting, detaching and jarring.

Honor thy father and thy mother. Lucky had always honored his mother, figuring out at an early age that she more than any other person on Earth was on his side. After he'd moved out, honoring his father became much easier because he could honor at a distance.

Until coming to the Selena rodeo, that is.

But humility comes before honor. For the first time, Lucky considered just who should experience this humility. He wanted it to be his earthly father, but, Lucky knew this time, yet again, it would be him. He picked up the phone. It took only two rings before Henry Welch barked a hello, managing to sound harried.

"Dad?"

"Your mother about to come home?"

No doubt Dad wanted home cooking.

"I don't think so. That's why I'm calling."

His father was silent, which was unusual enough to give

Lucky hope. But then, his dad was canny. He had to know something was going on.

"Go ahead," Dad finally said.

"I've met a woman here. Her name is Natalie Crosby."

Lucky heard a book close and a chair creak before his dad stated, "Crosby? That was Tisha's last name."

Surprised his father remembered, Lucky hurried on, "Yes, she's Tisha's cousin, and apparently she dated Marcus, too."

His father's snort indicated no surprise. Lucky winced. So far, he was making Natalie sound a whole lot like Tisha, and nothing could be further from the truth. Still, Lucky continued, wishing the words sounded better, wishing his gift of gab hadn't failed him at the worst possible moment. "Dad, she has a son. He's three years old. His name is Robby and—"

"She's claiming the boy belongs to Marcus?"

"She doesn't need to claim. One look at Robby and there's no doubt."

"There's always doubt," Dad insisted. "What does she want?"

Lucky felt the pressure lifting. "She doesn't want anything." It was true, too. Not once during their negotiations last Tuesday had she brought up money. He had, and she'd explained about the will, the missing money and then the discovery of the bank bonds.

"Dad, I'm just letting you know that here in Selena, you have a three-year-old grandson. His name is Robby Crosby. His name should be Robby Welch. Mom and I met him, and we already love him."

"You stay away from this woman, and tell your mother I said get home now."

"Dad, this is something you need to tell Mom yourself. But I'm staying in Selena. Robby is Marcus's child, my nephew, your grandson, whether you like it or not. I'm going to help take care of—"

Lucky needn't continue. His father had hung up.

Good thing, too, because Lucky might have accidentally given away that not only did he intend to become a permanent fixture in Robby's life, if his heart was any indication he intended to do the same in Natalie's.

Chapter Seven

Natalie felt even more lost on Saturday morning as she stood in the front doorway watching as Robby piled toys in the backseat. He was convinced that Miss Betsy needed to see his train collection. He was convinced Lucky needed to see his trucks and broomstick horse.

All Natalie really needed to do was toss in some food and clothes, and they'd be good to run away for at least a week.

She shook her head, clearing the cobwebs and fantasies. "Come in, Robby. We need to get a sweater on. It's cold."

"Nooooooooo."

"Yeeeeeeees."

While he truly believed that Miss Betsy and Lucky needed to see his toy collection, he didn't think Miss Betsy and Lucky needed to see his warm clothes. He chose cowboy boots, shorts and a torn white T-shirt. He wasn't happy when Natalie changed him into a warm red sweater and a pair of heavy-duty jeans. That she let him keep the cowboy boots went unnoticed.

"I hot," he insisted, so Natalie changed him into a long-sleeved T-shirt, tucked the sweater in his backpack and, finally, with only ten minutes to spare, buckled Robby into his car seat and crawled behind the wheel.

She imagined herself driving to Canada. It was a straight shot north.

"Mommy, choo-choo," Robby whined. Usually, Natalie worked hard not to reward such behavior, but this morning, no way did she want to show up at Bernice's with an unhappy, screaming kid and a disheveled look. She jumped out of the car and headed into the house to retrieve yet another train. She knew just the one he wanted. She'd put it on top of the refrigerator last night when Robby decided that playing on the kitchen floor with his train was more important than eating.

Hopping back in the car and handing Robby his beloved favorite train, she hoped he didn't do the same today. Natalie didn't need Mrs. Welch demanding an account of what, when and where Robby ate, and why he thought throwing himself on the kitchen floor was okay.

Bernice lived twenty-five minutes away, on the other side of town, in a house that looked lived-in. Natalie parked behind a red Sebring. Checking the child mirror, she saw Robby's anxious face and forced herself to calm down.

"We're going to have fun today."

Robby nodded and went for his seat belt. Since Natalie didn't want him to master unbuckling yet, she made it around the car and to his side quickly. To her relief, he ignored the stash of toys and simply held on to his favorite train. They'd barely taken a few steps when the front door opened and Lucky came out.

"The star attractions!" he called.

"You mean attraction," Natalie corrected.

Robby pulled his hand from hers and ran toward Lucky. "See my choo-choo."

"I see your choo-choo," Lucky said. "And, I meant attractions. We're glad that both of you are here. Come on in. Most everybody is either in the kitchen or around back."

Natalie had actually been here a few times as a teenager, but back then she'd been here for the horses and hadn't noticed the down-home look. It was a kid's dream. Scattered toys, soft furniture, and most breakables were out of Robby's reach.

Small things, but they helped Natalie relax.

She didn't need to ask Lucky directions to the kitchen. The aroma of fried chicken led the way. Then came the sounds of laughter and raised voices.

"Mary's here. Do you know her?" Lucky asked.

Bernice's oldest daughter, nine months pregnant and ever the high school cheerleader, raised a Popsicle in greeting.

"Everybody knows Mary," Natalie finally said as Robby pressed against her leg and herded her toward all the noise. Clearly, he wanted to be in the thick of things, only he wanted to make sure she was near. "I was three years behind her in school."

"Natalie!" Bernice turned from the oven when they walked into the kitchen. "I'm proud of you and mad at you at the same time."

"Mother," Mary warned. She was placing plates on the table. Natalie did a quick count—eleven.

Hmm.

Bernice aimed a large spoon at Mary and shook it. "I'm supposed to fade into the background, I've been told. Still, we're so glad you're here. Most everyone is in the backyard."

Lucky looked relieved to get out of the kitchen.

"I want kicken," Robby said. He headed for the stove.

Bernice blocked the oven door, spoon at the ready. "Well, of course you do," she said. "I've saved a leg just for you. I'll bet your mother's taught you the word *hot*. Am I right?"

"I think she has some six-legged chickens hidden away because she always offers legs to my two children," Mary added. "Rachel is Robby's age. Shall we introduce them?"

The backyard was even better than the living room. A swing set beckoned. The door to the barn was open enough so Natalie and Robby could see horses, hay and farm tools. Even better than that, right in front of the barn were the beginnings of something.

"What that?" Robby asked.

Lucky crouched down so he was eye level with Robby. "Howie Junior's been bugging me to help him learn to ride bulls. I put together a mini-arena. I've been making him jump on the bales of hay, and I've been helping him with balance. See?" Lucky pointed. He'd tied a metal barrel to four trees. "With just a pull on a rope or two, Howie gets to ride a pretend bull."

"Oh," Robby said. He'd stopped paying attention after the first three or four words. He took two steps toward the barrel.

"I don't think so," Natalie said.

Lucky shot her a look, but echoed, "I don't think so."

Robby looked ready to let out a healthy three-year-old whine, but luckily someone laughed behind them. Robby turned and saw kids his own age. He took two steps in their direction, looked at his mother questioningly, decided he was brave enough to leave her side and ran toward Howard, Bernice's husband, and Mary's two children. A little boy bigger than Robby stayed near his Grandpa, but a little girl just Robby's size ran toward him.

"Robby, wait!" Natalie called, but it was too late.

They met hard in the middle, looking like two tiny sumo wrestlers. Both fell to the ground. Robby sat up first, grinned and said, "Okay?"

The little girl nodded, "'Kay."

"I'm thinking about making her a bull rider," Lucky said after both children brushed themselves off and ran toward the swing set. Lucky smiled as the little girl scampered up the slide with Robby right on her heels. For the first time, Natalie noticed how his smile seemed to reflect in his rich brown eyes.

Lucky continued, "So far today, Rachel's fallen off a chair, hit her head on a door handle and pulled a bowl on top of her head. Not once did she cry. She did ask the bowl if it was "kay.""

"Rachel must be two."

"Yup."

"Robby was forever hurting himself when he was two. One night I heard him. He'd fallen out of bed. When I got to him, he was already back to sleep, on the floor, clutching a shoe. He had a knot on his head. I stayed by him for hours afraid that he shouldn't be asleep, but also afraid to wake him up."

"And Marcus missed all those things," Lucky said sadly.

"Yes, he did." There was no sense sugarcoating it.

"I just find that so strange." Lucky sounded amazed. "He loved children. When we were teens, he was the one who worked at a special-needs camp for three summers in a row. It had some kind of animal therapy with horses that Marcus helped with. The kids loved him. He still gets letters."

Natalie opened her mouth, but the words didn't come. She'd never really met Marcus, and Tisha had only had negative things to say.

"I still wonder. How did you meet?" Lucky started.

"Where's your mother?" Natalie interrupted.

Lucky sobered. "She's not here. I planned on telling you but was hoping to let you settle in first. We called my dad Wednesday after church. We told him about Robby."

Natalie's stomach clenched. Lucky's dad was the one who

knew high-dollar lawyers. Lucky's dad even scared Tisha. Tisha wouldn't say what it was about the man that frightened her. She left Natalie with the idea that not only did Marcus want nothing to do with his dad, but that his dad wanted nothing to do with them.

"Dad made her come home. He doesn't believe Robby is a Welch."

"And your mother went?" Natalie had trouble fathoming the concept.

"She went. I drove to Lubbock and put her on a plane Thursday. She cried the whole way."

"Oh, my." Natalie sat on a bale of hay.

"I promised her I'd take lots of pictures today. I hope you don't mind." Lucky took out his cell phone, punched a button and aimed it at the children.

It would be a lovely picture, Natalie thought. Mary's daughter's blond hair shimmered in the sunlight as she tried to climb up the slide instead of using the steps. Robby's brown hair stuck straight up in the air. He followed the little girl's lead. Looking back at Lucky, Natalie watched as his hand went to his own hair, smoothing it back, making sure it didn't stick up. The smile had gone out of his eyes. He was probably thinking about what his mother was missing.

Natalie had spent the day, the week, the last two weeks regretting what her rash announcement at the rodeo had done to *her* Robby, *her* world, *her* life.

She'd forgotten there were other people, other worlds, other lives involved.

And they were hurting just as much as she was.

Lunch went great, except for his mother's absence. Robby sat between Mary's children. He mimicked the older boy and bowed his head in prayer, even saying Amen, and then took care of little Rachel. Robby moved her drink so it wasn't too near the edge of the table. Lucky took a picture. Robby said "Nooooo" when she reached for Grandpa Howard's butter knife. Lucky took a picture. The little boy seemed to think he had a job taking care of Rachel, and he intended to do it. Lucky's mother would have been mesmerized. Lucky was. He hadn't been around kids much, except at the rodeos, and there they all seemed to want autographs or cotton candy.

Looked like Robby was a good kid.

Natalie relaxed after her second piece of fried chicken. It was only the second time Lucky had seen her without a pinched and somewhat panicked expression. He took another picture, this one of Natalie.

She'd almost relaxed with him Wednesday night during church, when he'd confessed that he was the baby of the family.

He caught Bernice's eye and smiled. This was her doing. Marcus had always accused Bernice of putting a truth serum inside her chicken because it seemed the whole family loosened up and came clean during one of her meals. Except for his dad, of course. Henry Welch had only made it to Bernice's table a handful of times during his marriage to Lucky's mother, and Lucky had grown up wishing Bernice's husband, Howard, were his father. Howard not only seemed to enjoy spending time with his family at the meal table, but also he wasn't above refilling a tea, cleaning up mashed potatoes from the floor or even doing dishes while his wife and her best friend simply sat on the front porch and talked.

"You going to stay at the ranch now that your dad's gone?" Howard asked Natalie.

"Yes. It's a perfect place to raise a kid. Plus, how could I leave? That place has been in my family more than a hundred years."

"Sure is a big house for one little girl," Howard said.

"Yes, but the little girl's lived there her whole life." Natalie didn't miss a beat. Lucky liked what he saw. She knew what she wanted, and she went after it.

He sat up and leaned forward, watching her face, her expressions, her mannerisms. She was a lady through and through. Amazing. And not Marcus's type at all. Natalie was Mary Ann. Marcus liked Gingers.

She continued, "Not much about the house or the land I don't know. I'm going to offer MacAfee more grazing land, and then the only thing I'll need to worry about are the four acres around the house."

Lucky watched the interchange. These were questions he'd wanted to ask, but didn't know how. When he'd first come to town—had it really only been two weeks ago?—everyone was talking about Natalie's lack of money.

Just last Tuesday, when he'd sat across from her at the diner, she'd let him know money was no longer a problem.

"Place the size of yours takes a lot of upkeep," Lucky said. He almost added that it would be hard enough for a man to take care of the grounds and chores, but he choked back the words. They sounded too much like his father's.

"For emergencies I have Patty and her husband. My dad's friend Walt calls almost every night."

"Uncle Walt gave me a lollipop," Robby added, letting them know that while he didn't follow the conversation, he knew it was going on.

"I like lolpops," Rachel agreed, nodding seriously. Mary's older son paid no attention to the conversation.

The fried chicken was that good.

Howard nodded. "There's not much about the financial dealings here in Selena that Walt doesn't know." Turning to Lucky, he said, "Walt owns the bank. He's turned the reins over to his son—"

"Who Natalie used to date," Mary interrupted.

"Lord, I forgot about that," Bernice said. "That was how many years ago?"

Natalie was blushing. "Too many to count."

Mary turned to her mother. "How many kids does Timothy have now?"

"Three, and his wife's pregnant with the fourth."

"Peter, Timothy's middle boy, is Robby's age," Natalie said. "We belong to a playgroup that meets every Monday morning. I haven't been since my father died."

"You need to go again," Mary said gently. "It's good to get out. I'd go nuts if not for the time we spend with friends who have kids my kids' ages."

Natalie looked at Lucky, and he saw her eyes go liquid.

"There's just been so much going on," she said softly.

"Some of it is good," Bernice reminded. "You're keeping the ranch." Then Bernice looked at Lucky and said, "Robby needs a father figure more than he needs other little kids. Who better than Lucky?"

"Mother!" Mary gasped.

Lucky might have gasped himself, but he was lost suddenly in Natalie's shimmering blue eyes.

"Mother," Howard said gently and looked at Robby. "Little pitchers have big ears."

Bernice took a bite of chicken and chewed while trying to, pretending to, look contrite. "Okay, okay, I've never understood that saying, but I know I promised not to interfere."

"What do you do besides the playgroup?" Mary asked. "My kids like it best when the toddlers from church get together. It only happens about every three or four months but—"

"I'm not a toddler." Johnny spoke for the first time.

Mary reached over and tussled his hair. "Of course you're not."

"Last summer we did the Mother and Toddler swim class. Robby was the best one there. He jumped in the first day. The lifeguard was impressed. If he could listen and follow directions, they would have moved him up a class."

"I a good swimmer." Robby held up his plate. "More?"

"I'll get you more," Bernice offered. "He has a good appetite, Natalie. What's his favorite meal?"

"Spaghetti, but he usually winds up wearing more of it than he eats."

"Johnny was like that," Mary said.

"Was not!" Johnny said it loud enough that both Rachel and Robby stopped eating.

"No yelling at table," Robby instructed.

"Table," Rachel agreed.

"One time," Natalie said, "when Robby was about eleven months and I wasn't looking, he managed to load most of his spaghetti into the back of one of his toy trucks. I noticed about two days later. Yuck."

Everyone laughed, and finally Lucky was able to tear himself away from her eyes. What he couldn't seem to do was forget Bernice's "father figure" remark. No one else seemed to be dwelling on it, though, not Natalie, and not Mary, who was laughing as she said, "Oh, Johnny did that, too, only with macaroni and cheese."

Johnny squirmed. "Did not."

Lucky shook his head. His mother had a similar story about both him and Marcus. She would have loved hearing what Natalie had to say. Bernice did a great job of making everyone feel comfortable. Still, she kept giving Lucky side looks, as if she blamed him for his mother's absence. Or maybe she blamed him for not jumping up and demanding more time with Robby.

He needed to assess what he was doing here. He'd made

his list, but despite the long-term on it, had he really thought beyond the next six months? The list only offered the basics. It didn't deal with just how much Lucky might want to *add* to the list.

Lucky put his third piece of fried chicken down and thought back to what Marcus had said about Bernice's chicken and truth serum.

In truth shimmering blue eyes made him want to stay in Selena as much as seeing Robby did.

"Lucky!" Mary said.

"What?"

"You're doing that staring thing again. You know, like you did when you were in high school and had better places to be than at our table."

"I never," Lucky insisted, "had better places to be than in front of Bernice's fried chicken."

Inviting Mary and her family was a stroke of genius on Bernice's part. Not only did having other young children make it more comfortable, but also as the meal continued on to dessert, Mary and Natalie shared a few memories. Natalie knew about Mary's exploits, and Mary knew about Natalie's barrel-racing skills.

By the time lunch was over, Rachel and Robby were nodding off, and Bernice was pushing everyone out the door so she could do dishes. Alone.

"It's easier," she insisted.

Natalie pulled Robby from his chair. He curled his arms around her neck and murmured, "Mommy, no sleep."

"Yes, sleep," Natalie said gently.

Mary was gathering Rachel up. Her blossoming figure didn't hinder her at all. "Let's put them on my mother's bed."

Lucky followed, watching the two women. Rachel was asleep; Robby was not. The moment Natalie laid him down, he popped back up. Natalie leaned over and whispered something in his ear. He looked at Rachel, nodded and settled into the pillow.

After she pulled the blanket over Robby, Natalie followed Mary out into the hall and managed a smile at Lucky.

"What did you whisper in his ear?"

"I told him to stay with little Rachel for a few minutes to make sure she's okay, and then I'll come and check on him."

"So he's not going down for a nap?"

"He'll be asleep before I make it to the bottom of the stairs."

About the time he and Natalie reached the back door, Johnny and Howie Junior were running toward the mini-arena. Mary trailed by just a few feet. Howie Junior turned on the radio and Van Halen blasted.

"You choose the music?" Mary asked.

"Yes," Lucky said, thinking he should direct his answer to Mary but unable to take his eyes away from Natalie. "When you're teaching young bull riders, 'Kum Ba Yah' just won't do."

Natalie put a hand over her heart. "I'm appalled."

"Honey!" Mary's husband called.

"Coming," Mary yelled. She studied Natalie and Lucky. "You two be good."

They both watched as Mary walked away, singing to the classic rock lyrics of Van Halen and looking every bit like she belonged onstage.

Lucky waited until she was out of earshot and shook his head. "That girl."

"Has a vivid imagination," Natalie agreed. "Give me a minute. I'm going to run upstairs. I promised Robby I'd check on him."

She hurried back to the house.

Lucky enjoyed the view. She didn't exactly run, more like scooted, and her shoulder-length hair bobbed with each step.

She told Robby she'd come back to get him, and even though she knew the little boy was probably asleep, she was keeping her word.

He admired that.

He knew the power of the Word. He'd taken on the role of preacher more than two years ago. First, helping his mentor. Then, filling in when no one else was willing or available. Finally, he'd stepped up to the plate, accepted God's calling and started organizing the services at the rodeos he attended. Cowboy Church filled a necessary void. Demand, not only among the rodeo participants, but also among the fans, increased every year. If he wanted, he'd have a pulpit, be it a tree trunk, every week, and he'd have listeners. Of course, Cowboy Church was nothing like the church here in Selena. Lucky sometimes wanted a regular church. Other times, the thought of trying to meet the needs of a diverse congregation scared him to death. Cowboy Church meant a certain breed of people. It didn't mean singing, one preacher, a chance to repent and then a prayer before goodbye. It meant lots of people coming forward and confessing their sins, both to relieve their hearts but also to encourage others. If there needed to be a baptism, they had to find a place to do it. Watching hearts heal had done a lot for Lucky because he'd seen firsthand what havoc loss of hope did to individuals, families, lives.

Maybe if Marcus had tried a littler harder, stayed with Natalie a little longer, then his life would have been different.

What little time Lucky had spent with Natalie certainly inspired him to want to try a little harder.

Stay a lot longer.

You two be good. He, unfortunately, had a vivid imagination, too, and wasn't entirely opposed to what Mary was thinking. Watching Natalie hurry down the back steps and toward him, he tried to remember that she was the mother of his *brother's* son. Instead of choosing the necessary path, the questions he needed to ask about Marcus and Natalie's past, Lucky queried, "You ever been here before?"

"Yes, but it's been years. Looks like they've done quite a bit to the place."

He started with the barn, noticing how she dragged her heels when they came near the stalls. He took her through the fields and down to a creek. At first, he talked about the land, comparing it to his grandfather's place. Then, he moved on to his career.

"Marcus always seemed to make the top fifteen. Me, I managed to stay in the top forty-five, which means, actually, that I made good money. Not as good as Marcus, but good enough to keep me in the game. This year, I'll be lucky to be in the top hundred. I'll probably break even this year. That is, if I don't skip any more rodeos where I've already paid the entry fee."

She shuddered. "I can't even imagine jumping off a bull."

As much as he wanted to, he couldn't tell her what she wanted to hear, because while she couldn't imagine jumping off a bull, he couldn't imagine doing anything else.

Yet.

"Most jobs are dangerous. We bull riders just have to acknowledge that the bull is bigger than we are and know how to get out of the way. It's the know-how that makes the difference. You take most people, they go to work, and if something dangerous pops up in front of them, they haven't any know-how."

He looked down at her.

"Nice try," she said. "But I design Web pages for a living, and there's nothing you can compare to the bull in my profession."

He grinned. She had him. Now, if she'd used her father's profession, owner of a stockyard, he'd have had an argument. If she'd used Howard Senior, or Mary's husband or…

"A computer could fall on your head. You could be electrocuted," Lucky offered.

"I use a laptop, it weighs eleven pounds. I also have a surge guard."

"I won't be a bull rider forever. Someday, I want to retire, have my own church and maybe a place like this." They'd circled the perimeter of Bernice's house. "I'm just not ready to throw in my hat, change my life, yet."

The breeze suddenly took on a colder feel, one that had Natalie studying him intently before turning back at the house. Lucky didn't know if it was truly the weather that clutched at his heart, his declaration that he could retire someday or the look on her face.

It was the first time he'd uttered the word *retire* aloud. He looked down at Natalie, blaming her for his change of heart, and noted how the top of her blond head came to just under his chin. He noticed how she kept her hands in her jacket pockets and how she watched Howie Junior and Johnny practice falling off the bales of hay. Funny, until he had Natalie at his side, he hadn't noticed how they always play-acted writhing in pain.

He wasn't ready to throw in his hat yet. But if he made Selena his home base, and he fully intended to, Natalie Crosby just might help him get there sooner.

Chapter Eight

Natalie looked out the window for the tenth time. Any minute now, per their agreement, Lucky would drive up and load Robby into his truck, into the car seat he'd borrowed from Mary, and off they'd go to church. Natalie would be in the house alone for the first time since her father's death. She could work on Web pages uninterrupted. She could sit in a comfy chair and read uninterrupted. She could maybe clean out a closet or two uninterrupted.

It was going to be a long, boring day, uninterrupted.

As if affirming her assumption, Robby crawled on the couch next to her and peered out the window, too. "Here yet?"

"Not yet."

"You come?"

"Not this time."

"Okay."

It was that easy for Robby to accept Lucky and a boys' day out.

Not that Lucky Welch could be described as a boy. No, he was a man, bigger than life, who was upsetting the applecart as her dad would say.

"Church fun," Robby remarked.

"I'm glad you think so."

Lucky's truck bounced into sight right then, and Robby was off the couch and tugging on the front doorknob before Natalie had time to smooth her hair and make sure her shirt was tucked in.

"Morning," Lucky called, stepping down from his truck and heading up the walk.

Yup, bigger than life. He wasn't a cowboy this morning. No, in a black suit, white shirt and gray tie, he was definitely a Sunday-go-to-meeting man. Natalie couldn't say why she was surprised. Maybe because on Wednesday night, he'd been relaxed in jeans and a flannel shirt. Looking down at Robby, she rethought his black jeans and blue sweater.

Lucky must have read her mind because when he got to the front porch, he said, "Robby looks fine. I'm all dressed up because this morning the preacher's wife called. Seems Tate's not feeling too good. They asked me to preach."

"Then Robby will be in the way. I can keep him home, and you can take him some other time." She'd meant to sound helpful instead of hopeful, but no such luck.

Lucky chuckled. "Mary's still in town. She's been bribing Rachel all morning with getting to see Robby again. She'd have my head if I showed up at church empty-handed. Robby will sit with them during the beginning minutes of service, then there's a children's hour."

"A children's hour?"

"Kids ages two to ten have their own service, down in the basement. There's puppet shows and singing."

Again, Natalie considered that the church Lucky was describing was not the church she remembered. It was more a church she wished she remembered.

Robby held out his hands, and Lucky picked him up. "You

weigh as much a baby bull," Lucky teased, hoisting the little boy high into the air. Then, he did something Natalie didn't have the strength to do. He flew Robby in the air all the way to the truck. Robby chipped in by making plane sounds. A moment later, Lucky deposited Robby in the child's seat and then started fumbling with the buckle.

"I do it," Robby offered.

"Oh, no, no, no." Natalie left the safety of her porch, where she'd been watching her son too willingly go off without her. She nudged Lucky aside and took the harness and first attached it at the chest and then between Robby's legs. She could feel Lucky practically pressed against her. She wanted to say, *Hey, preacher man, isn't there, like, a two-fingers rule about how close you can stand to the opposite sex?* But she knew he was just studying her every move, watching her buckle Robby in, so he could buckle Robby in safely, without her assistance. Knowing that, she didn't mind if he stepped on her toes.

Truth was, she didn't mind how close he was at all. He was warm and smelled of soap. The bottom of his chin brushed the top of her head. If he were anybody else, she'd think he was invading her space on purpose.

"We'll probably go out for lunch after services, so I'm thinking we'll be gone about three or four hours. Okay?"

"You'll need his bag." Natalie quickly returned to the house, grabbed Robby's diaper bag and hurried back to Lucky. "If he says potty, take him right then. We're getting it right about ninety percent of the time."

She almost wished Lucky's cell phone was within grasp. She needed a camera because the look on Lucky's face was priceless.

"Mary will know what to do," Natalie assured him, holding out the bag and almost enjoying his unease because it was so comical. "There's a diaper just in case, but I doubt you'll need it."

Lucky looked skeptically at the bag and didn't make a move to take it.

"Trust me, you need it."

Finally, Lucky took the bag. He placed it in the front seat.

"We go!" Robby urged.

"We go," Lucky agreed, slipping into his truck and into three-year-old lingo easily. He paused, then turned around to check out his backseat. Clearly having second thoughts, he said to Natalie, "You want to come with us?"

"To church?"

"That's where we're going."

"We go, Mommy!"

No, she didn't want to go to church. She didn't want to sit still for an hour, didn't want to answer the questions as to why she was suddenly attending and who she was attending with, and most of all, she didn't want to hear a sermon about sorting out right from wrong.

Because right now, Natalie was doing wrong. This preacher man deserved to know the truth: that Robby was Marcus's son but *not* Natalie's. The urge to tell him almost made her dizzy. It was the right thing to do. It was the scariest thing in the world to contemplate doing. She caught the handle of his truck in a firm grip. No way did she want to have to explain to Lucky exactly why she was feeling faint.

"Natalie!"

She looked up at him, blinked and opened her mouth. Words didn't come.

"You either need to let go of the door handle or, even better, jump in and come to church with us."

"Yes, Mommy, come church."

"No, I can't go to church."

"Can't or won't?" Lucky asked.

"Both work." She stepped away from the truck, surprised by how much she wanted to go with them. If only she'd borne Robby, if only…

Lucky started the truck, the wheels turned and he slowly drove away. He waved, and in the backseat, Robby tried to turn. The safety harness only allowed so much movement. Still, his little head bobbed up and down as he tried to see her while trying to wave, too.

Her knees almost buckled. Her little man was going off without her. Taking a deep breath, she regained her composure and looked back at the house. For a month, she'd been daunted by how empty it was without her dad. Empty didn't begin to describe how it would feel without Robby.

She took one step, two, back toward the porch. Actually, this was good. She and her dad had always agreed that Robby shouldn't be coddled, and since her dad's death, Robby had been nothing but coddled. At church, he'd be with Rachel, who at the moment was his favorite person, and he'd see Patty and her kids. Realistically, this was a good separation.

Good for Robby.

Not so good for her.

Glancing back, she watched as Lucky's truck got smaller and smaller. So this was what "shared custody" felt like, like a best friend moving away, promising to write, but it's never the same.

When the truck finally disappeared from sight, Natalie opened the front door and went in. Evidence of Robby was everywhere, more so now than when her father was alive. Back then, she'd tried to keep things picked up. Now, the toys lay at the ready, and in some ways it was a maze to get through the living room and to the kitchen.

With hours to kill, she started cleaning the living room,

worked her way to the kitchen and did both bathrooms, then her and Robby's bedrooms. The guest room simply needed airing out.

The door to her father's room had been closed for almost a month. It needed more than an airing out; it needed emptying out. Walt had offered to help more than once. Standing in the hallway, in front of the room that had belonged to her father, Natalie figured the room felt and looked much like she did, lonely and dusty.

She checked her watch. Church should be ending right now. Lucky planned to take everyone out to lunch. She'd love to be a fly on the wall for that venture. If he blanched at the diaper detail, he'd also be bewildered when Robby refused to eat, crawled under the table and wanted to run around greeting the other diners.

Pop Pop called Robby a future Wal-Mart greeter.

She had more than an hour. The knob turned in her hand and the door pushed open, almost without her consent. Lately, she seemed to be doing more things she didn't want to do than things she wanted to do.

She needed to change that.

Her father's scent of Old Spice and down-home comfort lingered in the room. She missed him. Oh, how she missed him. She'd never felt like a single mother with him by her side. She'd felt like a family. And three seemed such a great number. It had been she, her mom and dad, three. Then, it had been she, Robby and Dad, three. Now it was Robby and she, two.

Three was a much better number.

She stepped into the room, thinking she'd wash the bedsheets and then grab some garbage bags and start packing her father's clothes.

The phone saved her.

In the quiet of a house that had not three, not two, but one lonely individual, the phone was loud, distant and welcome.

She hurried downstairs and picked it up.

It was Lucky. "Robby's crying, and we can't get him to stop."

"Did he fall?"

"No," Lucky said slowly, "I went to pick him up from Bible hour, and when I peeked in, he was just fine. He was sitting by Rachel and holding up his finger and singing *'This Little Light of Mine.'* Rachel spotted Mary and ran right to her. Robby just looked at us, and when I told him to come on, his bottom lip quivered, and he started sobbing."

"Put him on the phone," Natalie ordered.

"Mommy. You no here."

Natalie knew just the expression Robby wore on his little face. He had eyes pooling with tears. He had a bottom lip that not only quivered but also stuck out. And he wasn't exactly crying, more like keening.

"Robby, what's wrong?"

"Mommmmmmy."

"Mommy's at home. You'll be home soon."

"Mommy home?"

Lucky took the phone then. Natalie had to give him credit for parental instinct. A phone call with Robby could take an hour and consist of mainly two-to-four-word fragmented sentences. Lucky, obviously, was too hungry to wait an hour. "Should I bring him home?"

"You can."

"Better still, why don't you drive over and meet us for lunch? We're going to The SteakHouse." She heard muffled sounds, and then she barely made out Lucky saying to Robby, "Mommy is coming to the restaurant."

"Eat!" Robby replied. No more keening, no more quivering bottom lip. "We go eat. Mommy eat."

She had no problem hearing Robby.

And she had no problem figuring out that the opportunity to say "yes" or "no" to the restaurant was gone. Robby missed her; Robby expected her at the restaurant. She'd meet them at the restaurant.

Part of her wondered if Lucky knew he'd worked it so she had no opportunity to decline the luncheon invitation.

Lucky came back to the phone. "It will take us about twenty minutes to get to the restaurant."

"Since it's Sunday," Natalie said, "you'll have about a thirty-minute wait. I'd call ahead, get your name on the list and then drive around a bit. Robby's a handful in a crowded room with no toys and no place to roam."

"Bernice already called, but I'll take your advice about driving around."

After she hung up the phone, Natalie looked down. She no longer felt lonely, but she still looked dusty. When Robby was a baby, she'd mastered the eight-minute shower. It served her well this morning. Unfortunately, there was no such thing as an eight-minute blow-dry. She took the full ten minutes needed, wanting to look nice, and worried that she was trying to impress the big cowboy more than the little cowboy.

Remembering what Lucky looked like, she chose an outfit she didn't get to wear often enough. Hmm, come to think of it, the last time she'd worn the black, satiny pants and matching black-and-white-striped jacket had been for an evening out back when Robby had been four months old and her father arranged the blind date.

That said something—her father trying to play matchmaker. The date liked Natalie, but he was about fifteen years too old. She'd never been willing to settle, which might be the reason she hadn't had a real date in three years.

Hurrying to the car, she checked her watch and figured she just might arrive in time for dessert.

But her hair would look great!

Natalie chuckled. Her father had bemoaned Natalie's attention to her hair. Of course, back when he was teasingly complaining, she hadn't mastered the eight-minute shower, and ten minutes would never do for a decent styling. For the first time in a long time, when she checked her image in the mirror, she felt like a woman more than a mother.

She could fool herself and say it was for Robby, but Natalie was no fool.

The day was taking a turn for the better, and maybe, just maybe, when she got back home she'd tackle her dad's room with a better attitude. Surely after a lunch with her little man, Lucky and Bernice's whole crew, loneliness would take a holiday.

In a way, the drive to The SteakHouse felt like a holiday. The weather was perfect, and Natalie was looking forward to being a part of something, something like a family. She turned on the radio and hummed along with a country station all the way to the restaurant.

The SteakHouse used to be a barn. It belonged to a family her father referred to as entrepreneurs. They had ten children and realized not all wanted to farm, thus the family restaurant.

It worked, Natalie remembered, as she pulled into the parking lot. Five of their ten children worked the land. Five worked the restaurant.

Natalie's timing couldn't be better. She walked into the restaurant just as Lucky and everyone were being seated.

"Mommmmmmy!"

As she stretched out her arms, Natalie overheard a diner say, "Kid sure is happy to see his mommy, but he looks just like his daddy."

Natalie's step faltered.

Every time she started thinking she could do this, share Robby, something reminded her that at heart she was, indeed, an only child, and she didn't share well. Worse, the diner's words, *"Sure looks like his daddy,"* reminded her that what she wasn't sharing didn't really belong to her in the first place.

Robby skidded to a stop and held up a piece of paper. "Look, Mommy. Look what I made."

It was a white piece of paper with cotton balls and craft sticks glued to it.

"Um, that looks really nice," Natalie said, guiding Robby to the table and helping him into the booster chair. Rachel was in a booster chair also, across from Robby, and she was holding on to a similar piece of paper.

Johnny, feeling the power of being the oldest, solemnly filled Natalie in. "We had a lesson in Bible hour about being sheep."

Natalie looked at Robby and made a quizzical face. "I thought you wanted to be a horse."

"No, sheep. Baa."

Everyone laughed. The hostess showed up, passed menus around, and before Natalie had time to worry about Robby's behavior, she found herself sitting between him and Lucky, who'd pulled out her chair. Robby was making a liar out of her by behaving like a little adult. He held the kids' menu as if he were reading it. Rachel did likewise.

Lucky leaned over. "You've eaten here before?"

"Many times."

"What's good?"

"You'd better say everything," the waitress walked up and said. She was still tying her apron. After she finished the knot, she retrieved a tablet from her pocket and said, "Is this all one check?"

Bernice said no; Lucky said yes.

It only took a wink from Lucky to encourage the waitress that one check was all that was necessary.

Natalie was impressed.

So impressed that she had a hard time keeping her eyes off him while he led the prayer. She noticed that he watched her, too, while she cut Robby's hamburger into small pieces. Luckily, little Rachel then insisted that Natalie cut hers and no, Mommy wouldn't do, it had to be Robby's mother. Natalie not only cut the meat but also arranged it in a happy face. She then made sure Robby ate six bites of his hamburger, three fries, and drank his milk.

When the last dessert was cleared away and Robby finished his milk, Bernice's husband stood. "We need to be getting home. There are still chores to do."

Howie Jr. was the only one to groan. Mary's husband, casting a worried look at Mary's bulging stomach, pulled a sleeping Rachel from her chair. Robby put down the toy train Natalie had pulled from the diaper bag and scooted to the floor. Natalie retrieved the train, Robby's sippy cup and two crayons from the table before taking Robby by the hand.

"Need help?" Lucky offered.

"No, I'm going to get him home and put him down for a nap. I have some work to do."

"Need some help with the all that work? Or better yet, how about if I come along and distract Robby after he wakes up?"

Natalie opened her mouth, but no words came out.

Her cell rang, saving her from making a decision.

Lucky tucked Robby under his arm, snagged the backpack from Natalie's hand and mouthed, *I'll wait for you outside.*

It was nice to have help.

Natalie flipped open her phone and listened to Sunni's normally calm voice rise a few octaves.

"Slow down," Natalie advised.

Over the line, she heard Sunni take a breath. Then, the lawyer said, "Natalie, the private detective just called. He started with Tisha's last known address and has been working his way backward."

"Has he found Tisha?"

"No, but he found someone else."

Lately, Natalie had gotten use to imagining worst-case scenarios. "Another baby?"

"No, he found another private detective."

Chapter Nine

Monday morning when the alarm clock rang, Natalie rolled out of bed with purpose. She'd tossed and turned all night, and in the gloom of midnight had made a decision. The private detective she and Sunni hired had not located Tisha. The private detective her father had hired had not found Tisha.

At least now they knew where her father's missing money had gone and why he'd put his business at risk. His private detective charged sixty dollars an hour plus expenses. Natalie's father had paid for airfare, hotel bills, gas…the list went on. It added up quickly.

And still no Tisha.

Her dad's private detective did know why he'd been hired. When Natalie's dad heard that Marcus had died and how much money Marcus had, he'd worried that Tisha might come around. He, like Natalie, intended to do everything in his power to keep Robby with them.

Her father's main goal, like Natalie's, had been guardianship papers.

Both Sunni and Natalie agreed. The private detective

needed to keep looking for Tisha. Until all parties came to an agreement, Robby's future was at stake.

The minute Tisha was located, Natalie was telling both Robby and Lucky the truth.

It was the responsible thing, the right thing.

She tugged on gray sweats and a pink T-shirt. Then she checked on Robby, grabbed a glass of milk, snagged a handful of cookies and headed for her office. The world as she and Robby knew it was about to change, and it was important for both of them to keep some things the same.

Like routines. Their routines had been disrupted when Pop Pop died. Then, their routines had been completely destroyed when Natalie challenged fate and lost. If she were honest with herself, she'd known Lucky was a good guy, which was why she'd approached him for money. But she'd never expected Lucky to turn out to not only be a good guy with a good family but also a good guy who wanted to be part of their lives.

Natalie booted up her computer and opened her calendar. So far the e-mail about her father's death had garnered lots of sympathy from her clients. All claimed to understand if she was a bit slow with updates, but a month had passed, and even the most patient of clients had to be having second thoughts. She'd been slowly getting back into routine; today was the day routine returned for good.

First, she sent out a blanket e-mail letting her clients know that she was back in the saddle and to please send new updates. She also attached a sample trailer, a cost breakdown, and offered her clients what she called "a new opportunity." She'd managed to catch up on just two clients when—

"Morning, Mommy!" Robby stood in the bedroom door, grinning. Clutched in his left hand was a pair of fresh, clean pajamas he'd gotten from his dresser drawer.

"Good morning, my favorite little man. I am so glad you're awake. You wet?"

"Uh-huh."

Ten minutes later, Robby sat at the table in jeans and a sweater, eating a waffle, or pretending to eat a waffle—one bite didn't really count as eating—and looking out the window.

Natalie looked out the window, too. Robby, she knew, was hoping for a cowboy. Natalie was hoping for a miracle.

Too bad she didn't believe in miracles.

"Mommy? What we do today?"

"I thought we'd go back to playgroup."

Robby's eyes lit up. "Playgroup? Yeaaaahh!"

The playgroup they belonged to met at the community center. Natalie had missed so many sessions she no longer had a current monthly calendar. After cleaning up the breakfast dishes and bundling Robby into a coat, they left the house. Robby insisted on walking by himself, climbing into the car seat by himself, and even trying to buckle.

Any other day, she'd feel proud. What an independent little guy, and was he growing up! Much too quickly. Today she wanted that small hand in hers. She wanted to smell the baby shampoo in his hair. She needed to know that she was the most important person in his world, the one who put batteries into trains and bandages on boo-boos, the one he'd call for in the middle of the night.

But what was best for Robby?

The community center was down from the church. Robby sat up straight as they drove past. He held up his finger and twirled it. "Little light of mine," he sang over and over. He looked at her, as if expecting her to join in, but she didn't know the words. She managed to hum the tune a bit as they pulled into the parking lot of the community center and

parked. Robby was still singing when she pushed open the
door to the preschool room. She ushered Robby in and to a
seat. Today, seven toddlers sat around two tables while parents
or caregivers helped them trace their hands. Two stopped
what they were doing, put their finger lights in the air and
started singing.

Natalie shook her head as she watched Jasmin, Allison's
little girl, glue eyes to her turkey. Would Robby be that careful
and artistic when he hit four? Right now his turkey looked
more like a ham, and it looked like green would be the color
of choice. One of the assistants was reminding the children
about the pilgrims and the first Thanksgiving.

Thanksgiving!

The kids were making turkeys because, of course, Thursday was Thanksgiving. She'd had her calendar open this
morning and hadn't even noticed. Patty had invited her weeks
ago. Had she said yes? Better make a phone call and soon.
Luckily, holidays were on the long-term portion of Lucky's
list.

Robby dropped his green crayon and grinned at all the
"Robby!" and "Hi, Robby" greetings he received. He even
received one "Hi, Thawobby." Playing the strong—make that
short—silent type, he neglected to do more than give a tiny
"Hi" in return. The lady in charge touched Natalie's arm in
welcome. Funny, up until two weeks ago, Natalie assumed
every touch, every nod, every tearful look was an act of
sympathy because of her father. Now, she worried that they
knew something else.

Which was why Natalie needed to deal with it before
someone said the wrong thing in front of Robby.

He'd gone to her place, but she wasn't home. Yesterday,
she'd been about to invite him over. He knew it. Whoever was

on the phone had upset her. He wanted to know why because his gut feeling was that right now everything that was upsetting her in some way, shape or form came back to him.

They had to get past this.

He found her at the park next to Selena's town square. She was sitting on a bench dividing her time between reading a paperback and watching Robby.

Lucky sat down next to her, enjoying her look of surprise, but then feeling empty when her eyes darkened to suspicion.

She'd been pleased for all of a nanosecond.

He didn't have time to ask why.

"Lucky!" Robby launched himself into Lucky's arms. Lucky stood, twirled the boy and then chased him across the playground. Lucky realized his mistake two minutes into the game. Sitting astride a bull was an eight-second ride; chasing a three-year-old was a much lengthier investment of time and energy. By the time Lucky climbed the slide, slid down, circled the swing set and jogged twice around the length of a park that rivaled a football field, Robby finally fell to the ground giggling. Lucky landed beside him. When Robby's giggling stopped, Lucky heard an echo. No, not an echo. What he heard was Natalie laughing at him.

Okay, so he was a bit winded.

Standing up, he managed to limp toward Natalie. She'd put her book down because he and Robby were much more entertaining.

"Again?" urged Robby.

"Oh, Lucky's got to rest," Lucky said. "You play on the slide and in a minute, I'll join you."

"I wish I had a camera." The November wind whipped Natalie's hair across her face. She brushed it back and looked up at him. The sting of winter put red in her cheeks, but still the laughter didn't quite reach her eyes.

"And I wish I had an eraser."

"What?"

"I wish I had an eraser so I could get rid of all your suspicions about me."

She shook her head. "It would need to be a pretty big eraser."

"I'll buy it if you'll use it," Lucky offered.

She looked up at him, somewhat frightened, but also managing a brave smile. He went down on one knee in front of her and said, "Natalie, I promise. We can make this work out so everybody's happy."

She nodded, silently, and then waved Robby over. "It's time for his nap. You offered to come over yesterday. If the offer still stands, how about today?"

"Best offer I've had all day."

Natalie's house hadn't changed since his first visit, except this time the "Welcome" on the front mat was literal. He followed her into the living room, where she turned on the television before ordering him to sit down. Then she and Robby marched up the stairs because Robby had announced in the driveway, "I wet."

Lucky followed orders, because resisting orders might result in him assisting with diaper duty. He sat down in what was definitely a man's room: beige walls, tan carpeting and heavy, brown leather furniture. The walls displayed a hodge-podge of pictures with no definite design. Some were of family, primarily Robby and Natalie. Standing, he started walking the room, really studying the pictures, the lives depicted on the walls. He saw Natalie as a small girl, in pigtails and missing teeth. He saw Natalie and her parents—she looked like her mother—in studio poses. Then he saw Natalie with Robby and Natalie's father.

They looked happy.

Interspersed between the family photos were the pictures of the property, from the beginning when it was a true working ranch to today when it, at best, could be called a house on a very large piece of unused property.

It seemed a waste. Natalie had mentioned her father's love for this land. She'd mentioned how the earliest house resembled an outhouse. It took him a minute, but he found the picture she'd been describing and almost laughed. She'd nailed it. Based on size and design, the first house had all the earmarks of an outhouse. The people of this era cared more to preserve land than faces. If an ancestor of Natalie's appeared, they were in the distance, on horseback or leaning against a fence. He glanced out the window. She still had plenty of room for horses and such. Really, this place was about the same size as Bernice's. It could easily be a working ranch again, maybe not Bonanza, but definitely a smaller version of Southfork. He looked at the pictures on the walls again. Nope, not a single one of Natalie on a horse.

They existed; he knew it.

He turned off the television. On Monday afternoons, soap operas, judges and home shopping salespeople ruled. Lucky'd rather live in an outhouse than watch.

Actually, he'd rather think about the lovely Natalie Crosby, who, by the way, muttered. The whole drive over here, she'd been talking to herself. From his vantage point directly behind her, he could see an occasional nod of her head. Every once in a while she made gestures, both fists of anger and then one quick open hand signifying exasperation. In the backseat, Robby's head turned right or left. He didn't seem to care that his mother was having a virtual conversation. Robby knew that Lucky was following them. Obviously, Robby intended to make sure Lucky didn't get lost.

Lucky had no intention of getting lost, ever.

After a moment, Robby and Natalie came down the stairs. Robby headed right for a leather chest in the corner of the room. He pulled out two or three trains and immediately started changing the look of the room. The oversize coffee table became a world with trains and accidents. He immediately started having a conversation. Lucky figured he was the recipient, but he definitely wasn't needed.

Natalie headed for the kitchen. "You can come with me if you want. I'm making peanut butter and jelly."

The kitchen looked a lot more like it belonged to Natalie. It didn't have the heavy browns of the living room, but more hues of burgundy and pink. It fit her personality. It smelled of cinnamon and Kool-Aid. It wasn't the smell, though, that made him look twice. It was the woman, standing at the counter opening a jar of peanut butter.

She took bread from the cupboard and started talking, almost more to herself than to him. The apple didn't fall far from the tree. "Before my father died, we had Robby pretty much potty trained. In a matter of days, right after the funeral, he was back to having accidents and wanting his bottle."

"Makes sense," Lucky said. "After Marcus died, I was all messed up. I wasn't hungry. I couldn't sleep. I kept waiting to hear him snore or have him wake me from a solid sleep because he suddenly remembered a joke."

"I thought you guys had stopped traveling together."

"We had, but when he was alive, it was like I knew he was out there somewhere snoring, saving up jokes to tell me. When he died, I knew it would never be the same again. There was this empty feeling I couldn't seem to get rid of. I think it was then that I really understood why some people give up hope."

He watched her, waiting. Surely she'd flinch, look sad, or something. The memory of Marcus's death should inspire some emotional response from her.

Nothing.

Not a tear, not a dirty look, nothing. She didn't mutilate the sandwich bread or fling jelly.

Nothing.

"Eat!" Robby ran into the room before Lucky could start to question.

"Yes, we're going to eat," Natalie said calmly. "Why don't you help set the table."

Robby headed toward the pie safe and took a handful of paper plates. Lucky followed the boy and watched as he set the table. "Pop Pop sat here." Robby pointed to where Lucky would be sitting.

"Thanks for letting me know."

"Otay." Robby ran to the counter, holding out his hand, and then dashing back to the table once the sippy cup full of cherry Kool-Aid was secure in his grasp.

Lucky took his seat, make that Pop Pop's seat, and waited. If he were a bit more comfortable, he'd be helping with napkins and drinks, but there was something disquieting about knowing he was sitting in Pop Pop's chair and doing what Marcus apparently never got to, *maybe never wanted to do.*

Robby picked up his sandwich and took a bite. Natalie stared at hers.

"Maybe we could say a quick prayer?" Lucky suggested.

"Okay," Robby agreed.

Natalie didn't bow her head, but she didn't object. Lucky made it short and easy. "God, thank you for this food. Amen."

"Amen," Robby echoed.

Robby took over the conversation. Good thing because it didn't look like Natalie intended to talk much. She stared out the window while Lucky listened to Robby talk about Lucky's truck—he wanted to ride in it again; to Robby talk about playgroup—he was glad they were going again; and to Robby talk about "Tanksgiving"—the boy liked turkey.

"Where are you going for Thanksgiving?" Lucky asked.

Robby looked at his mother; an exaggerated expression gave away that he knew the word *Tanksgiving* but not the meaning, yet.

"We're going to my friend Patty's." She finally focused on what was in front of her. Maybe what she was seeing out the window was not the wind in the trees but the past.

"Patty's," Robby echoed, like he really knew. "For turkey." For the rest of lunch, Robby turned his peanut butter sandwich into a train and then a horse. Lucky followed suit by turning his peanut butter sandwich into a plane and then a bull.

Natalie managed a tiny smile before reminding Robby that if he didn't eat his sandwich there'd be no treat.

"For you, either," she told Lucky.

"And you," he responded pointedly.

He and Robby finished their sandwiches in record time.

When the last crumb was accounted for and the last potato chip put back in the bag, Robby scooted from his chair and took his paper plate to the trash.

"Mommy, nooooo," he immediately whined.

"Robby, yes," Natalie countered. Looking at Lucky, she said, "It's nap time and because you're here, he really doesn't want to go."

"Nap time! Wow, I wish I could take a nap," Lucky said.

Robby didn't look convinced.

Glancing at Natalie, Lucky suggested, "How about if I go with you two? I'd like to see your room."

Robby's eyes lit up. "I have choo-choo room."

The stairs creaked under Lucky's weight. Robby made it to the top first with Natalie right behind. It didn't take a genius to figure the positioning was on purpose. If Robby tripped, Natalie would stop the fall. Judging by the three-year-old's sure-footed scampering, falls didn't happen often.

"Hurry," Robby urged.

Robby's bedroom, like the kitchen, showed Natalie's touch. Trains ruled. "I started with Winnie the Pooh," Natalie said, "but when Robby got old enough to choose, it quickly became apparent that he liked trains."

Robby climbed in a train tent and choo-chooed for a minute. Then he scooted out and hopped on his train-shaped bed.

"Under the covers," Natalie ordered.

"But—"

"Under the covers," Lucky echoed, surprising himself. His words surprised Natalie, too, judging by her expression. They worked wonders on the boy, though. He crawled up to the top of the bed, put his head on the pillow, pulled up the covers and closed his eyes.

Then, he opened one.

When he saw they were both still in the room and still staring at him, he giggled and closed it again, this time covering his head with the blanket.

"Go to sleep," Natalie ordered.

"Lucky here awake?" Robby peeked out.

"I don't know if Lucky will still be here when you wake up," Natalie said, "but if you don't go to sleep, I'm asking Lucky to leave now."

"Go to sleep," Lucky echoed sternly.

"Otay."

This time he closed his eyes fiercely and pretended to snore.

And Lucky knew he intended to be there when Robby woke up.

* * *

Closing the door to Robby's room, Natalie turned to Lucky and said, "Go on downstairs. I have one thing to do and then I'll join you."

He left without arguing, continuing to be the one sane, reliable person in her world. She leaned her head against Robby's closed door.

Changes were coming, and if Lucky was any indication, Robby would benefit. There existed a family who was so thrilled with the little boy they'd probably bring a boxcar into their backyard if Robby wanted it.

"Natalie." Lucky's voice was low. He was standing at the bottom of the stairs.

"Can you see me?" she whispered.

"Yes."

Great. First of all, what man can hear a whisper? Her father certainly never heard her whisper, but then, he was hard of hearing. Natalie had called it his selective hearing. Worse, since Lucky had answered yes, it meant he'd been watching her lean against Robby's door.

She turned, heavy hearted, and headed for the stairs. When she reached him, he didn't move. He simply said, "Are you all right?" She was forced to look up at him, feel his warmth, and he was warm. He made the house feel alive again, like when her dad moved through the rooms.

No, she wasn't all right. Her world kept spiraling out of control, and everywhere she turned, here was this man offering to make it better, offering to help. The kicker, what made it all so frustrating, was that not only was he the most willing to help, but also he was the most qualified. "I'm all right," she finally said. "I was just thinking about all the decisions I have to make."

He nodded, and it looked like he started to reach for her

but stopped himself. Natalie wanted to sit on the bottom step and cry. Since meeting Lucky, time and time again he proved that he was someone she could rely on, lean on.

"When I woke up this morning," she admitted, "I decided today was the day I'd tell Robby about his relationship with you."

He smiled and she noticed that he was one of those guys who had a half smile. She'd never realized just how appealing half smiles were.

"Good," he said. "Can I help?"

She led the way to the kitchen; he willingly followed.

"Natalie," he said when he sat across from her at the kitchen table. "You know what I like best about you?"

She looked at him suspiciously. "What?"

"You bounce back good," Lucky said.

Natalie blinked. Her father used to say that, until she fell off the horse that last time. "What?"

"You bounce back good. No matter what life throws at you, you meet it head-on, and no matter what, you're keeping Robby as the most important aspect of your life. I admire that."

She swallowed. If this were a Lifetime movie, she'd be the one with the secrets, the one the audience pushed to tell the truth. She was the one lying, Lucky was the hero, and every day he seemed to grow even more heroic. Yet here he was saying he admired her. Truth was, she didn't bounce back; she fell flat.

"How well did you know Marcus?" Lucky asked suddenly.

"Not well at all," she admitted.

"Did you love him?"

"No, I didn't love him." In some ways, though, she was starting to have warmer feelings toward Marcus. Surely any brother of Lucky's couldn't have been all bad.

"Why didn't you?" Lucky asked slowly.

"He belonged to Tisha," Natalie said simply. Desperately, she tried to think of a way to change the subject.

"Would you even know Marcus if not for Tisha?"

Natalie shook her head.

"Marcus used to be my hero," Lucky admitted. "He could do everything, and he did it well. He made the top forty-five in just three years. I'm in my sixth and still haven't gotten there. This might have been my year, but truthfully—" his grin disappeared "—my heart's not in it."

She wanted to say, *Tell me about your brother.* But that would give her away. Even more, she wanted to say, *Tell me about you.* Still, he'd finally given her a chance to change the subject. "Why did you become a bull rider?"

"When you're not raised on a ranch, bull riding's the event to get into. Neither Marcus nor I had the hours in the saddle to become a bronc. We're city boys."

"You don't act like a city boy."

"That's because we spent summers with my grandparents over in Delaney. Grandpa had us in the saddle, but two months every summer didn't make cowboys out of us."

She understood. For years, Allison's mother gave riding lessons. Natalie and Allison had watched as kids here for two-week vacations thought they were *riding* horses. What they were doing was holding on to horses, usually *holding* on to the saddle horn like it was the only thing between them and the ground. In most cases, it was.

"I'll bet you were a natural," she said.

"Marcus was the natural, and Grandpa had been a bull rider. He had us on barrels from the time we were little. I could show you pictures. Made my mother worry and my father threaten to keep us home summers."

"But still you became a bull rider."

"I think my brother and I did everything we could to do exactly the opposite of what my father wanted."

"I loved riding," Natalie said. Boy, had it been a long time since those words had come from her mouth. "Dad was what you'd call a more-than-gentleman farmer. His dad ran a working ranch, and so did my great-grandpa before him. Dad remembered when this place really thrived. But the 1940s were really hard, and my great-grandpa started selling off parcels. My grandpa managed to keep it as a working ranch, but even he had to sell off a few plots. He realized that if anything was going to remain for his two sons, he'd need a career change."

"The stockyard?" Lucky said.

"Yup. Grandpa managed to buy back a few pieces after the stockyard made good. Dad took over after he got out of college. He married my mother and almost immediately started buying horses and a few cows. Mom kept chickens and, from what I hear, she was partial to mules."

"When did your mother die?"

"I was eight. Dad got rid of the chickens, cows and such because without her help, he just didn't have the time. He kept the horses. I was already a big help taking care of them."

"What about your uncle, Tisha's dad?"

"Dad bought Allen out. It's kind of a sad story."

"What's he do for a living?"

"He works on his wife's family's dairy farm. He still has five children living at home. He…" Natalie stopped. Just how much did she tell Lucky? If she opened her mouth, used Tisha's name, wasn't she getting that much closer to saying something she'd regret, something she wasn't ready to share?

Oh, what a tangled web we weave.

"Natalie?" Lucky encouraged.

"Allen's never been known for having much luck in life."

"Are all his kids like Tisha?"

Natalie had to give Lucky credit. Most people, once they'd met Tisha, had all kinds of opinions. He asked the question everyone thought but didn't have the courage to address. He even managed to look thoughtful.

"No, none of the other kids are like Tisha. She, like your brother, was the oldest. She took off at eighteen, and I don't think she's ever been back."

"So, she had a rough childhood and that's why she's the way she is?"

"What she had was a childhood without all the extras and without happiness. They just never had money. I'm not sure her parents even had the desire for things like cable or designer jeans. She came to spend the summers here, at my dad's request, and when it was time for her to go back home, she'd cry and cry."

"Because you had cable and designer jeans?"

"Cable, designer jeans, entry fees for rodeos and all the fast food we wanted just a fifteen-minute drive away."

"She came every summer. Were you friends?"

"Friends? No, not really. I had friends, Patty and Allison. Even more, I had my dad and I had horses. Dad wanted to keep me from being lonely, but I was never alone. I think by the time he realized that her spending the summer with us wasn't good for me and wasn't good for Tisha, he didn't know how to stop it."

Lucky scooted his chair closer to the table and reached across to touch the top of her hand. "I think every family has issues. Some work them out as a family. Others never work them out."

She nodded, noticing that his hand remained on top of hers, noticing how light his touch was, how caring.

Who was she? Was she someone who could work through

this with Lucky? Or was she someone who would never work it out?

Was she like Tisha?

Looking across the table at Lucky Welch, Natalie again realized the power of a lie and how much a lie cost everyone involved.

For a while, she'd only thought of losing Robby, but now she realized that once the lie escaped, she'd be losing Lucky, as well.

Chapter Ten

It was a two-bedroom apartment with horse privileges. If it were any other place, it might have worked. The bedrooms were small; he could live with that. The kitchen and living room were combined. No problem. The bathroom only had a shower and not a bath. Again, no problem. The only problem, besides that it was the second story of a barn and his comings and goings would be public because this was a working ranch, had to do with the rancher's wife. The landlord, Richard Dunbar, was friendly yet all business. He discussed responsibilities, price and lease. No wonder this was one of the more successful cattle and hay ranches in the area. He also mentioned having seen Lucky at church.

For a moment, Lucky was convinced he'd found temporary lodging. He couldn't stay at Bernice's forever.

Then Patty Dunbar had entered the apartment. A curvy blonde, whom Lucky remembered well from the rodeo and from church, she was Natalie's best friend—something Lucky hadn't realized when he saw the ad in the paper. She was also a mama bear. Natalie didn't need any help; she'd been taking care of Robby just fine for three years. He had everything a little boy would ever need.

With a baby on her hip and a single purpose, Patty demanded, "So why are you thinking about signing a six-month lease? You have the travel trailer. Selena, Texas, is not a central location for a bull rider. Surely it's about time for you to be heading out again?"

"I'll get to the rodeos," Lucky assured her, even though he now had no intention of renting the place, "and it's time to settle down."

"Honey, I think I hear someone crying," Richard Dunbar suggested.

Patty gave her husband the I-know-what-you're-trying-to-do look and said, "If that were true, I'd be hearing the sound and not you."

"Maybe this is a bad idea." Lucky put his hat back on and stepped toward the door.

"Yes," Patty agreed.

Lucky almost smiled, but he didn't think Miss Patty would appreciate it. Too bad Richard Dunbar hadn't provided a last name during the phone query Lucky made, but then, why would he? Richard provided directions and agreed to meet Lucky at the barn. They'd been in the apartment all of five minutes when Lucky heard a screech, which was followed by someone pounding up the stairs.

"Look, Mrs. Dunbar, I didn't realize this was your place and I'll tell you what I keep telling Natalie. I only want to help."

Richard looked lost. He opened his mouth as if to say something, then wisely closed it.

A wail came from down below. It was followed by a "Mommy, I fell!"

"Wolf in sheep's clothing," Patty muttered before taking off.

Richard waited a moment. "I probably owe you an apology. I knew my wife wouldn't consider having you for a tenant, but I've been mulling something over for the last couple of days and it involves you. When you called, I figured it was God giving me the go-ahead."

"The go-ahead for what?"

"I've heard you preach," Richard said. "I mean, besides this past Sunday. It wasn't at that Cowboy Church you're so involved in. It was at a little congregation in Van Horn, with barely twenty-five members."

"I remember." Lucky remembered all too well. He'd gotten little sleep, had to drive more than two hours round-trip on top of preaching, and when he finally got on the back of his draw—a bull named ThrowAway—he'd made just three seconds. "A friend of my mother's attends there. She got my mother to ask me to preach. I about broke my neck trying to get everything done that day."

"I was visiting my cousin." Richard motioned toward the apartment door. "Let's head downstairs. I was only there that one day. My cousin doesn't attend church, so I went to the congregation closest to his house. I was in for a surprise. You gave a great sermon."

"Thanks." Lucky followed Richard out the door and down the stairs.

"So, whether or not you're renting this particular apartment, you're still settling down in this area?"

"Yes, absolutely."

Richard shook his head. "Most of the town didn't know Marcus was Robby's father. I'm not sure Natalie's father even knew. Judging by my wife's behavior, she knew. She'll also get over it if you do right by Natalie."

"I plan to."

"Good." Richard headed for the house with Lucky following. When they reached the bottom step, Richard turned around. "Have you given any thoughts to renting in Delaney?"

"No."

"Come on in. I'll get us some iced tea, and I have a proposition for you."

"Are you sure your house is safe?"

Richard laughed. "Patty's bark has always been worse than her bite."

"She threatened to hit me with her purse at the Selena rodeo. I'm thinking she has more heavy-duty weapons here."

"The iced tea is cold, and Patty makes the best chocolate-chip cookies this side of Lubbock. I'll go lock up her purse. You coming in?"

"I guess with that kind of incentive, I'd be a fool to say no."

Patty had one of her kids sitting on the kitchen counter. She was putting a bandage on his knee while he cried and said, "Ooooww. Oow. Ow." The baby crawled on the kitchen floor, seemingly fascinated by an errant paper towel.

Richard headed straight for the kitchen, said a few words to his wife that Lucky couldn't hear and then came back carrying two glasses of tea and a plate of cookies.

"Good balance," Lucky complimented him.

"Comes with helping the wife with the kids."

Lucky took one of the teas and followed Richard's example by sitting down, taking a drink and then placing his tea on the coffee table.

The living room was about the same size as Natalie's, but this living room showed a successful marriage of two styles. There was still an abundance of browns, tans and beiges, but here there were also frilly lamps, watercolors on the wall and no heavy furniture. The couch was red.

Richard took two cookies, offered one to Lucky and sat

back. "Patty tells me that your mother was one of the Selena rodeo queens and that your grandparents lived in Delaney."

"I spent summers in Delaney."

"You still have friends there?"

"No, not really."

"Still like the town?"

Lucky thought back to the too-enthusiastic sign, the café and general store, and the playground. He thought about the empty church. "Yeah, I still like the town."

"I'm an elder here. Did you know that?"

"No, my mind's pretty much been on other things since I arrived."

Richard nodded. "I can sure understand that, but there's going to be a time when things settle down, much like you're planning to settle down."

Lucky leaned forward, took another cookie and said, "Mr. Dunbar, why don't you just say whatever it is you're trying to say."

"The church in Delaney has been without a minister for five years. Some of the men of the congregation tried to keep things going, but they all work long hours and, besides preaching on Sunday morning, none of them had the time or the know-how to do all the other things a preacher does. The church is in good condition."

"It's a historical landmark," Lucky remembered.

"For the last three years, many of its members have driven all the way to Selena to attend services. Others, though, have stopped attending altogether. There's a whole community hurting for a local congregation, and we can't seem to find someone to put behind the pulpit."

"And," Lucky said slowly, "you think I'm the one. As much as I appreciate the suggestion you're about to make, I'm a bull rider. Sundays are not a day of rest for me."

Richard leaned forward and, in a voice much too decisive, said, "Your brother was the bull rider."

Lucky leaned back. Nothing like having someone malign your talents after they offer you a job preaching. "No." Lucky shook his head. "I'm not ready to give it up yet. This would have been my year if my brother hadn't died. I'm in good shape, only a few injuries this year—"

Neither Richard's expression nor posture changed. "I've seen you and your brother ride. You've got a good seat, Lucky, I'll give you that, but with bull riding, you either give it your all or you give it up. I've never seen you give it your all."

"You've got a point—" Lucky stood "—but, as you said, I've got a good seat. Now I just need to ride better. I'm not ready to quit, and I don't think you can judge my skill on what you saw at the Selena rodeo."

Richard looked like he wanted to say something else, but a soft "ahem" came from the doorway separating the living room from the kitchen.

"I've overstepped," Richard said. "I tend to do that when I get excited about an opportunity, and I think you're just what the church in Delaney needs. You'd help restore a lot of souls. Surely that's more important than buckles and purses."

"I'll keep your offer in mind." Lucky finished his tea in one gulp and headed for the door. He may not have been hit over the head with a purse, but he'd been hit over the head with an offer. The offer packed more of a wallop.

As Lucky jumped in his truck and started the engine, he couldn't help but think that God was telling him in more ways than one that it was time to really think about his future and where his priorities were.

What he'd done in the past was good, but maybe not good enough.

Maybe that was the kind of bull rider he was.

Good, but not good enough.

His worry, though, was maybe he was that kind of preacher, too.

Good, but not good enough.

"Mommy, I hungry."

"Hmm," Natalie said noncommittally. She glanced in the rearview mirror. Robby should have fallen asleep the moment they left Patty's. No wonder. He'd missed taking a nap; he'd played almost nonstop, and he'd been cuddled and hugged by every adult there. Patty had a huge family, and they'd always counted Natalie as one of their own. Richard's family wasn't quite as big as Patty's, but what they lacked in numbers, they made up for in size.

Natalie's Thanksgiving had been something else. It had been melancholy. She'd sat in Patty's living room and laughed with the family. At Patty's table, she'd bowed her head in prayer and this time she understood why. She'd eaten the traditional turkey, stuffing and pumpkin pie. She'd played Monopoly with the young people, and she'd taken Robby to the potty.

The whole time she couldn't shake the fact that in her entire life, this was the first time she'd not celebrated Thanksgiving at home.

A home that now felt so empty.

"I'm so full I can barely fit behind the steering wheel," Natalie said. She turned the windshield wipers on as a gentle rain began.

Robby giggled.

"How can you be hungry?"

"I no know."

Glancing again in the rearview mirror, she couldn't help but enjoy the sight of Robby grinning at her. His hair was a mess, and he'd spilled something blue on the front of his shirt, but oh, was he happy.

"Good day?" she asked.

"Good day," he mimicked.

"Do you want to stop at the café and have some ice cream?" The rain increased. It was almost a perfect end to a busy day. Rain meant staring out windows, touching paned glass and waiting for a rainbow.

"Ice cream, yeah!"

The family who owned the café up until two years ago never opened on major holidays, but some out-of-staters had purchased it, and now the blinking neon light didn't seem to recognize the Sabbath or holidays. To them, Thanksgiving was just a day at the cash register. Natalie might grump about progress, but today it didn't keep her from taking a prime parking spot and hoisting Robby out of his seat and inside. She let go of his hand for just a minute while she shrugged out of her coat. That was all it took.

"Lucky!" he shrieked, and across the diner he went.

He had a clear shot since the diner was pretty much empty. Lucky Welch sat in a booth by himself, eating a turkey sandwich and reading the Bible.

He looked up just in time to catch Robby to him, and then he uttered words that only cemented what Natalie already knew. They'd be joining him.

"Looks like my prayer's been answered." Lucky grinned.

She was an answer to a prayer. Wow. Well, at least Robby was an answer to a prayer.

"I'm glad you're here. I was feeling pretty lonely."

"Can't have that," Natalie said.

"Did you get my message yesterday?"

"The one inviting Robby and me to church?"

"That's the one."

"I got it." Natalie stared out the window. Rain tapped the glass, giving her an excuse not to look at Lucky. "I've been busy catching up with work, and I've also been cleaning out my dad's room. It's past time."

Lucky was silent as he took the last bite of his sandwich. "I had to clean out Marcus's trailer."

"My dad's boots were on the side of the bed. His glasses were on the table. There was even a shirt tossed on the end of the bed. The room looked like it was waiting for him to come back."

"Yeah, I know that feeling, and it's harder around holidays. Did you go to Patty's?"

"Yes," Robby said, sounding all the world like a little grown-up.

"Why aren't you at Bernice's? They always have a huge Thanksgiving." Natalie snagged a menu from between the ketchup and mustard bottles and stared at it. No way was she going to order food, but she was having a hard time not staring at Lucky. If she kept it up, he might notice that she was staring *with interest*.

"Mary went into labor. The whole family packed up in ten minutes flat and were out the door. They invited me to come with them, but I've spent more than my share of Thanksgivings in hospitals."

"Mary's in labor? Why have you spent Thanksgivings in hospitals?"

"Hospitals?" Robby repeated.

The waitress showed up at that moment, took both Robby and Natalie's ice cream order. When she left, Robby took the salt shaker and stuck it in his mouth.

"Robby, no." Natalie took it away, and Robby screamed.

Lucky looked surprised.

"This is parenthood, too," Natalie said. "It's not all grinning boys in car seats and playing at the park and getting hugs." With that, she scooted Robby from the booth and took him outside. The crisp November air was a slap in the face and just what Natalie needed. She'd overreacted in there a tiny bit. Robby was acting like a typical three-year-old who'd missed his nap. She was afraid of getting too close to a man who threatened her lifestyle in more ways than one.

"Mommy, we stand here? Get wet?"

"We're standing here getting wet because I'm about to put you in the car and drive home. You don't get to scream in restaurants. Do you hear me? If you scream again we're going home."

He nodded, but then, he nodded a lot. Sometimes he nodded when she told him the man in the moon liked green peas. One time he nodded when she told him she was going to buy him pink cowboy boots with pretty sequins on them.

Lucky was eating the last of his mashed potatoes. He was also doing that half-smile thing that disarmed her the other day.

"So," she said, sitting down and returning to the conversation exactly where she left off, "Mary's in labor? And why have you spent more than one holiday in the hospital?"

"Mary's in labor. Nobody's worried. I expect there will be a new grandbaby any minute, and, Natalie, think, what do I do for a living?"

"Oh, yeah."

"What you do?" Robby questioned.

"I ride bulls."

"Oh, yeah."

Robby's "Oh, yeah" sounded exactly like Natalie's. Lucky choked a bit on a spoonful of mashed potato, and then burst into laughter. Robby did, too. Laughter that brought tears to his eyes and also brought the waitress running to make sure everything was okay. Finally, Natalie allowed herself to laugh.

"That sounded good," Lucky said when everybody finally settled down.

"Robby's 'Oh, yeah'?" Natalie asked.

"No, you laughing. I don't think I've heard it before. You know what they say?"

"What do they say?"

The ice cream arrived as Lucky flipped his Bible open. "Here, in Ecclesiastes, it says, *'There is a time to weep and a time to laugh.'*"

"I've heard that line before," Natalie said.

"Good, that means you're open to the Word."

"I don't know about that." Natalie stirred her ice cream for a minute, not taking a bite but not pushing it away. Sometimes what she wanted wasn't good for her.

Like Lucky.

"I just happened to hear that line somewhere," she finally said. "I don't remember where. Probably television."

"I've been sitting here studying the Word. The answers have always been here. Many are in Ecclesiastes. Solomon also says there is *'a time to be born and a time to die.'* I've been angry with God for letting Marcus die. But he didn't *let* Marcus die. Marcus chose a dangerous profession. Every bull rider knows the risks. I was angry at God, and I was angry at Marcus. Truth is, I just need to grieve."

"My father was too young to die," Natalie said. "And he wasn't in a dangerous profession."

The doctors mentioned cholesterol as the major cause of his heart attack, but lately Natalie had wondered if worry about Tisha, about what would happen after the private detective found her, had somehow contributed.

Maybe Tisha contributed to Natalie's father's heart attack.

The thought had rocked Natalie's world one more time.

"Is it in the Bible, the phrase, *'And the truth will set you free'*?" Natalie asked.

"I know that one by heart. John 8:32."

"So it really is in the Bible?"

"It really is." Lucky reached across the table, took her hand from the ice cream she wasn't eating and covered her fingers with his. His palm was rough, but there was that warmth again.

"Mommy, you 'kay?" Robby asked.

"I'm okay." Natalie wanted to jerk her hand away from Lucky's, but the truth was, she liked the warmth there. She liked the thought that he kept reaching out to her, wanting to help.

"Mommy, mo ice ceam?" Robby broke into Natalie's thoughts, reminding her what truth she was hiding and why. Her little man wore more ice cream on his face than was left in the bowl.

"You're right," Natalie told Lucky as she pushed her dish of ice cream over to Robby. He'd have a killer sugar rush, but she needed him to be quiet, entertained. She needed to talk with Lucky.

Lucky tapped his Bible. "He said it first. I just repeated it."

"Money," Natalie whispered. "I've never been in want. After Dad died, it was the first time I ever really worried about what it would be like without it." She looked up at Lucky. "It's what drove me to you, asking for help."

"I'm so glad." The half smile returned in full force. Lucky bowed his head. It took Natalie a moment to realize he was praying. With his hand resting on top of his Bible, he was praying. She looked at his Bible. It obviously meant a lot to Lucky. It was dog-eared and pieces of papers marked pages.

"What were you praying for?" she said when he raised his head.

"I was actually thanking God for sending you and Robby here. I'm glad Mary went into labor and I wound up eating here with you and Robby."

He looked at her. "You're why I'm in Selena."

"Robby's why you're in Selena."

"Maybe at first."

Funny, the whole time at Patty's, she'd felt like there was someplace else she was supposed to be. Here, at the diner, she didn't have that feeling. Natalie looked at Lucky's Bible again. "What does He say about sharing children?"

Lucky laughed. "When we first met and everything was going so fast, and you were so afraid and I was so mad, I turned to the Bible. The first story I considered was about Solomon. Two mothers were claiming a child to be theirs. Solomon pretty much said to cut the child in half and let each woman have a part."

"You're kidding," Natalie said.

Even Robby looked interested, like he was following the story.

"No, not kidding. Solomon was a very wise man. The true mother said to give the child to the other woman, to spare his life. The woman who was not the mother said nothing. Thus, Solomon knew who to give the child to."

"Maybe we need Solomon."

"Maybe," Lucky agreed.

"Who Solman?" Robby asked. He really wasn't interested in Natalie's ice cream; right now he was more interested in playing with it.

"A very wise man," Natalie said. Lucky's spoon inched over, and he snatched a spoonful of Robby's ice cream.

Natalie took her spoon and helped herself to Robby's ice cream.

"Moooommmm." He snatched up his spoon and took a quick bite and then another and another.

It was gone in a matter of moments.

"Fun, Mommy, this fun."

"Marcus never ate all his ice cream," Lucky said. "It always went to waste. But if I tried to take it, he'd gobble it up."

"You have lots of good memories with Marcus, don't you?"

"Yes. To me, he was larger than life. Your friend Patty's husband made me realize something this last Tuesday."

"Patty told me you looked at her apartment. I told her to rent it to you."

"I'm considering something else now. Anyway, Richard offered me the church in Delaney, and when I told him I wasn't a pulpit minister but a bull rider, he said, 'No, Marcus was a bull rider.'"

"You're a great bull rider. I was mesmerized at the rodeo."

"Great? No. Good, yes. I am a very good bull rider, but not like Marcus. Growing up, I did everything he did. I wonder if he ever got tired of a little brother tagging along. Don't get me wrong, I love bull riding, but I wonder…would I be a bull rider if not for Marcus?"

"You would have been. Something like that, it's in your blood. You can't fake it." For the first time in years, Natalie thought about what she'd given up when she'd refused to get back on her horse. Maybe if she had, she'd be remembered for what happened after the fall instead of remembered for the fall.

"The sport's changed so much since I was barrel racing. I almost fell off the bench when I saw the first bull rider wearing a helmet instead of a cowboy hat."

Lucky chuckled. "Change is good."

Natalie slowly nodded. "Some change." She rearranged Robby, who was now falling asleep. "That being said, and since this little guy is telling me it's time to go home, let me tell you what else I've been doing since Monday. I've been reading articles on the Web about telling children the truth about their heritage."

Lucky's eyes lit up. It looked like he was about to say, *And you're going to tell him?* but he looked at Robby and instead said, "What have you decided?"

"Seems like the experts agree. Trying to keep the truth a secret is unrealistic over time. It's traumatic to the person hiding the truth, and it can harm the person who doesn't know the truth." She looked down at Robby. "Harming him is the last thing I'd ever do. I thought about telling him Monday, but so much happened that day. We went to the library Tuesday, and I checked out books about this. I've been reading them to him at night and emphasizing how special he is. I'm ready to tell him tonight, while you're here with us."

"He's asleep," Lucky pointed out.

"He's dozing. He's not all the way asleep. I can tell by his eyes. Robby, sit up."

"Otay, Mommy."

"Robby, you know how Lucky's been hanging around a lot, trying to get to know us, being our friend."

Robby nodded.

"Well, he's going to be around a lot more."

"Otay."

"A lot more, Robby, *for you,*" Natalie emphasized.

Robby nodded again. "Otay."

"Look over at Lucky. Notice how he looks a lot like you?"

Robby was through nodding. She had his interest, and while he wasn't understanding everything, he was understanding enough to know something important was going on.

Lucky started looking uncomfortable. "Maybe we should be somewhere else, like a counseling office or with my mother or something."

"I thought about the counselor," Natalie admitted, "but

Robby knows you, he likes you, and adding a stranger to the mix would only take away from what we're trying to tell him." She pulled Robby onto her lap, noticing how big he was getting, and how soon he wouldn't fit on her lap while they sat in a booth. "Lucky is your daddy's brother. You know, like Patty's children are brother and sister."

Robby no longer looked sleepy. He stared at Lucky for a long time. Then he leaned back against Natalie. "He Daddy?" Robby questioned.

"No, he's your uncle," Natalie responded. "A very special uncle.

"Not daddy?"

"Not daddy," Natalie said again. "He was your daddy's brother."

"Sometimes," Lucky said, "uncles act like daddies."

"Daddy," Robby tried the word. Then, he nodded again. "Daddy for keeps."

Chapter Eleven

"Yes, I'll be careful. No, I won't be gone long. Yes, I'll come right over to see you when I get back." He was talking to Natalie, but she was merely acting as a go-between for Robby. Robby had all the questions, but they were in a three-year-old lingo that Lucky still needed help translating.

Robby finally got on the phone and said his own, "Bbyyyyeee."

"Bye," Lucky said.

Natalie took the phone as Robby ran back to the kitchen to grab a snack. Not even Lucky could compete with the cookies they'd just made. "He talked about you all the way home. He's not bothered by the truth a bit. He thinks it's great to have a daddy for keeps. I'll work on the uncle thing while you're gone."

"This time I'll only be gone for two days. You know, when I first found out about Robby, I skipped a few rodeos. I felt like I had to. Now that Robby knows I'm his uncle, his special uncle, I really don't want to be away. This weekend, for the first time, I really want to skip rodeos. But I've already paid the entry fees. Although I've been hit or miss this year, there's still time to earn some money, at least break even. Plus, with Cowboy Christmas Week coming up—"

"Cowboy Christmas Week?"

"The busiest week a bull rider has. I've paid entry fees for more than twelve rodeos, and they all happen in just five days. None of them are next to each other. Usually by this time, I'd either have a driving buddy—" he paused and Natalie knew that he was remembering Marcus "—or I'd have arranged plane fare when I could still get it cheap."

"Where are you going?"

"This morning I'm flying to Greeley, Colorado. I'll ride this afternoon and then either catch a ride or hop a flight to Steamboat Springs, Colorado. I'll ride Saturday night, and then I'll somehow find a red-eye from there to you. I'll stop by Sunday morning, take you two out for breakfast, before church. You will go with me?"

"I'll think about it."

"Have you taken a look at my Bible?"

Natalie thought about the book sitting on the table beside her bed. Last night, Lucky had carried a sleeping Robby to the car, buckled the boy in with a little assistance, and as he held open the door so she could easily slide into the front seat, he'd handed her his Bible.

"Take this home," he'd said. "Look at some of the passages I've highlighted. You'd be amazed at how much they help."

She started to hand it back, but he closed the door before she could.

He sure had a way of getting her to do what he wanted. First, getting to know Robby. Next, coming to church. Now this Bible thing. "I've looked at a few passages," she admitted. "It's more interesting than I imagined, but it's also confusing."

"I'll help you understand the confusing parts. Now don't say you'll think about it. Say you'll go with me."

Her heart sang. *Say you'll go with me*. He wanted both of them. Then, she stilled. Her heart had no right to sing. Yes, telling Robby the truth had somewhat set her free, but she had one more secret.

Lucky rambled on, "We'll discuss Robby, my parents and some other things. I'll be home for four days, and then the show begins. The truly good news is that the first rodeo I'm entered in for Cowboy Christmas Week is in Odessa."

"Why is that good news?"

"Because you and Robby can come."

Natalie didn't answer. She couldn't. She heard the exuberance in Lucky's voice, all because he wanted them to attend, and suddenly she wanted, more than anything, to be there with him.

"I have a hard time at rodeos," she said, hedging for time.

"I know, but I'll be with you."

Natalie paused. *I'll be with you*. That seemed to be the dominant theme of most of the scriptures Lucky had highlighted.

"Okay, I'll really think about it," Natalie agreed.

Then Natalie had another thought. She'd screamed in both excitement and terror while watching Lucky and the others ride their bulls during the Selena rodeo. She's been fascinated, but she hadn't cared for any of them.

She definitely cared for Lucky, so much that it was starting to hurt. "Tell you what, I will go to church with you Sunday morning, breakfast, too, and I promise to think about the rodeo."

"Robby loves the rodeo."

"You're going to have to come up with something better than that," Natalie teased before saying goodbye.

She thought about the rodeo as she took Robby to the park and then over to Patty's for a Friday-night movie. She thought about it Saturday morning while she worked on Web sites, signed on two new clients, and even did a keyword search for Tisha. She thought about it while she made Robby breakfast and started both laundry and dishes. She thought about it when the doorbell rang and Robby, a little boy in footed pajamas, ran in front of her to open the door. They were greeted by the local florist who was actually delivering flowers himself.

Roses.

Red and white.

From Lucky to her.

Oh, wow.

"I don't usually deliver flowers myself, Natalie, but after writing down the message on this card, I just had to follow through."

"Writing down the message?"

"Yes, most times when I'm filling out the cards for people online or over the phone, it's just the standard message. You know, 'Thanks for a wonderful evening.' 'Thinking of you.' 'I'm glad you're in my life.' Your young man, however, gives quite a message."

Natalie took the flowers, pulling a section of baby's breath off for Robby, and then opened the card.

I've never wanted a home until I met you and Robby. Every day I'm on the road, I'll be thinking of you and counting the minutes until I come home. Remember what the book of Ecclesiastes says in the third chapter: There is a time to love and a time to hate. Thursday night I realized it was time to love—and I'm falling in love with you. Yesterday morning, I realized it was time to hate—I hated leaving Selena and you and Robby. Call me Lucky in Love.

"Wow," Natalie said.

"I usually only allow thirty words, but I got so busy listening to your cowboy that I let him go over. Not sure what I would have cut, anyhow."

"Mommy! It broke!" Robby's baby's breath was shredded. Natalie pulled another section off, handed it over and after setting the vase on a table went to get her purse for a tip.

She realized she was still holding the card as she watched the florist drive away.

"Wow."

Before this went any further, before her heart was fully vested, she needed to tell Lucky the truth. She had a feeling, however, that for her heart it was already too late.

Colorado had been cold, cold, cold. Lucky took fifth in Greeley and third in Steamboat Springs. The cowboys who'd teased him about going to Selena instead of Lubbock were no longer teasing. They were too intent on keeping their standing, knowing their place in line, and Lucky was no longer in the line. No matter how he scored, he wasn't going to be in the top forty-five. It was too late. At most, if he sat down and tabulated his winnings, he'd find the earnings equal to his spending.

And he didn't care.

He intended to finish out the year, do one last Cowboy Christmas, and then if the position at the church in Delaney was still open to him, he was taking it.

"Your toes okay?"

"Doc said I broke two." Lucky opened one eye and checked on Travis Needham. The boy had wasted no time after getting his feet wet in Selena. Apparently, he'd been doing a rodeo near Colorado Springs while Lucky had been doing Greeley, but they'd wound up next to each other in Steamboat Springs.

"Don't worry. If I had to break something, it might as well be toes."

Travis nodded, and Lucky wondered if the boy really understood that bull riders rode with broken ribs, collapsed lungs and fractured skulls. Lucky thought about telling him, but didn't. Travis wouldn't listen. Lucky hadn't. Marcus hadn't.

"What time do you think we'll land?" Travis asked, looking out the window of the Cirrus SR20. They'd lucked out and met up with a wealthy cowboy out of Abilene. He'd fly them to Abilene, and then they could rent a car or catch a bus to Selena.

"We've got decent weather except for this wind," Lucky said when the small plane hit turbulence. "I'm thinking maybe four or five in the morning."

"I hate the bus. I took it from Lubbock to Colorado Springs. I thought I'd be saving money, but all I did was lose time and money. The bus was so late I almost missed the rodeo."

"Yeah, the bus definitely is a last resort, but we'll only be three hours from Selena, so it won't be that bad. We'll get home around eight." That would give Lucky enough time to get to Natalie's, take her and Robby to breakfast and then make it to Sunday school. He'd be exhausted but happy.

Travis was already exhausted and happy. He'd come in last at both of his rodeos, meaning he got on the bull, wrapped his bull rope around his left hand, shouted "GO!", burst out of the chute and promptly lost the bull and found the ground.

After an hour of listening to Travis relive the rodeo, Lucky closed his eyes. His toes hurt, and he needed to sleep because he wanted to be wide-awake during his time with Natalie and Robby.

At best, it was a guarded sleep.

The sun had no intention of making an appearance in Selena this late November morning. It was a gray-and-black dawn. Travis's dad was waiting for them at the bus station. He shook Lucky's hand and took Travis's bag. His "How'd you boys do?" was answered with a solemn "Placed third and fifth" from Lucky, followed by an enthusiastic "Dead last, Dad!" from Travis.

Travis's dad dropped Lucky off at Bernice's and drove away. Dark, gray clouds filled the sky and seemed to reach for the ground. One ray of blue sky heralded their way. Lucky stood in Bernice's front yard a moment, thinking that for one bull rider a beginning lay ahead, but for him, he'd reached the end.

Bernice had given him a key when she realized he planned on staying. She wouldn't hear of letting him hook his travel trailer up to the barn and live out there.

"How'd you do?" Howie Jr. jumped up from the kitchen table and all but ran Lucky down.

"I did good, third and fifth."

"Why didn't you come in first?"

"I broke two toes in Greeley, still stayed on. The toes still hurt in Steamboat Springs, and I still did my eight seconds. Guess my form was a bit off, though. I slipped two spots."

"You want breakfast?" Bernice asked.

"No, I'm going to take a quick shower—" he glanced at the clock "—quicker than I like, and then I'm picking Natalie and Robby up."

Bernice beamed. She was worse than his mother in some ways.

He showered, dressed and was out to his truck in just twenty minutes. It was another twenty minutes to Natalie's house, and she was definitely worth the effort. Natalie answered the door, dressed in a silky red dress that emphasized curves and invited him to imagine the future. A future for the three of them.

Yes, he could spend forever with this woman.

Natalie stayed by Lucky all during church. Already he seemed to know everybody, and everybody seemed to know him. Some of them seemed intent on emphasizing that they were from Delaney and mentioned the drive. They all either shook Natalie's hand or hugged her. She'd never been hugged so much in her life. Robby, on the other hand, liked getting his hand shook, but he wound up with even more pats on the head.

Sunday school was easy. Lucky found a class for newcomers, and the preacher himself was the teacher. It was a small class. There probably really weren't that many beginning Bible students in Selena. In many ways, Selena, Texas, could be called the starting point, or maybe the stopping point, of the Bible Belt. It depended on which way you were traveling.

This morning's topic was the prodigal son. Natalie almost wished the preacher had attended the birth-order class. It would have been interesting to marry the older son to the characteristics of a firstborn, and the younger son to the characteristics of the baby.

When class ended, Natalie was surprised. It had been an hour but felt like minutes.

"What did you think?" Lucky asked. He took her arm and guided her out into the hallway.

"Interesting and painless," she answered.

"Painless?"

"I've always figured church was boring. I'm just surprised that it's not."

"The Word is never boring." Lucky looked a bit forlorn.

"Sometimes it's painful, knowing family members are lost and such, but there's hope for those who seek."

They fetched Robby from class and took him to Children's Bible Hour. He was in his element, unable to decide whether he wanted to sit with Patty's kids or Mary's. He chose neither and sat right between two older girls who thought he was cute.

"He's a charmer," Lucky whispered.

"Like you," Natalie whispered back. She almost giggled when he stopped in his tracks.

They stopped at Selena Café after church. The waitress brought the correct drinks without being asked and didn't even blink when they ordered four bowls of ice cream. Then, without even discussing it, they went to Natalie's house. While Natalie changed into jeans and a T-shirt, Lucky, mindless of his good clothes, carried out the boxes containing her father's stuff. He stored them in the back of his truck. He knew some retired bull riders exactly Natalie's dad's size.

The minute he was done loading the truck, Robby insisted on a movie, which he fell asleep halfway through. Lucky carried him to bed.

When he came back downstairs, he sat next to Natalie on the couch. It reminded Natalie of high school and first dates and how good it felt to be nervous.

Lucky definitely made her nervous. Especially after that card had said he was falling in love with her. Neither of them had brought it up yet, but the chemistry between them was electric.

"I'm leaving Thursday night," Lucky said, gazing at her. "I'm taking my travel trailer. Travis Needham's going with me. That gives me three days to be with you and Robby. I've got two things I need to do. One, find a place to live, and two, deal with my father."

"I'll help you pick out a place to live," Natalie offered. "I think Patty will be a little more open to renting to you now."

"I was thinking," Lucky said slowly, "about heading over to Delaney."

Natalie was silent. Patty had already told her about the offer of the Delaney church, and more than one church member this morning certainly had mentioned it.

"Delaney's not that far," she said softly.

He put his arm around her, pulling her close, and whispered, "Could it be you don't want me that far away?"

"Could it be I want you even farther away?" she countered.

"I don't believe it."

"Good, because it's not true."

Lucky laughed, didn't remove his arm, and said, "Finding a place to live probably isn't the biggest issue. If push comes to shove, I can rent from Patty for a while, or even stay with Bernice a bit longer, and then take my time picking out a place in Delaney if everything works out. I've never been a pulpit minister, and quite frankly, the thought terrifies me."

"If it terrifies you, why are you doing it?"

"Because God is calling me to."

"You've been doing Cowboy Church for years. Why are you terrified?"

"Cowboy Church is me preaching to peers. And, really, there's very little for a preacher to do. Most of the time it's anybody who feels like it either witnessing or confessing. Their problems are no surprise. I've lived their problems. In Delaney, I'll have to do funerals, baptisms and weddings."

"Weddings," Natalie whispered. "I never imagined you doing weddings."

"Basically, I'll be a servant to every member of the church, whether I understand the way they live or not."

"You're a natural," Natalie encouraged. "Look how well

we're doing, and what a start we had. When I met you I wished you off the face of the Earth, and today…"

"Today…?"

"Today," she said slowly, amazed at the words and how much she wished them to be true, "I wish I'd met you four years ago."

"I wish that, too," he said.

"But then I wouldn't have Robby."

The silence that followed should have been uncomfortable, but it wasn't. The flowers Lucky had sent were on one of the end tables. The red and white petals delicate, joyful. Everything could be right, *if only*. For a minute, Natalie worried he'd bring up Marcus, ask the all-important question that had simmered under the surface for weeks. *If you didn't love Marcus, how did you have his child?*

Next time he asked, she would tell him the truth. She was just happy that he wasn't asking today.

"Robby's a big reason for needing to meet my father head-on. This is killing my mother, and she doesn't deserve it. My father has acted irrationally more than once. There's no excuse for his behavior."

Natalie didn't have a response because if Marcus had been an involved father she'd not be a mother.

"Anyway," Lucky continued, "I was thinking about driving to Delaney tomorrow, and I wondered if you'd come along. I want to check out the church and see if there are any rentals."

"If you're willing to go later in the day, we'll go," Natalie said. "I'm working hard on catching up my Web business. I took too much time off after Dad died."

"Would eleven be good?"

"Delaney's just an hour away," Natalie said. "How long were you thinking of staying there?"

"Two or three hours."

"If we leave at eleven, we're talking about being gone during Robby's nap time. He's usually—"

"How many hours do you work?"

"I try to put in five hours a day."

Lucky thought for a minute. "Let's go at eight. I'll get us back here about two. Robby can go down for a nap, and when he wakes up, I'll babysit until you've done your work."

It was like being with her dad again, organizing their lives so both of their needs were met. It was a feeling of not being alone. She could get used to it.

"Tuesday," Lucky said, "I'm taking on my father. I don't care where it happens, here or there. We're going to add Grandma to Robby's life with or without Grandpa."

"Are you flying to Austin?"

"Maybe. You wanna go with me?"

"No, I'm not ready for that."

"Then I'll try to get them here."

"Oh, goody."

"Natalie, I admit, I'm not sure taking you to meet my dad is a good idea, but I'm thinking that once he meets you, he'll have to realize just how wonderful you are."

"I'm not wonderful."

He shook his head. "Just look in the mirror. All you'll see is wonderful."

Skeptical was too tame a word to describe the look she tried to give Lucky.

He responded with the familiar half smile, before sobering up to say, "You're right, though, it might be too early to introduce you to my dad. I'll fly out alone on Tuesday morning and fly back Tuesday night. What do you want to do on Wednesday?"

"Me? What do I want to do?" She was surprised by the

question. Lately, she hadn't been doing anything but planning on how to get her life back to normal.

There was nothing normal about Lucky Welch, brother of Marcus Welch, asking her what she wanted to do on Wednesday.

"Are we starting to date?" she asked carefully.

"I hope so."

"It's happening awfully fast."

"Not fast enough," Lucky said. "I've already admitted how I feel about you."

"There's a lot you don't know about me."

"I'm going to enjoy finding out."

"What if you find out something you don't like?"

"We'll work through it."

Yeah, right, Natalie thought. Before she had time to dwell on the seriousness of the conversation and its repercussions, he went on, "We're doing what I want on Monday. Tuesday I'll be gone. Let's do something you and Robby would like on Wednesday."

"Like look for a Christmas tree?" Her eyes lit up.

"Hey," Lucky cried, hugging her close. "You're making me feel, well, like Santa. I've never really looked for a Christmas tree," he said. "I'm assuming you're not talking about going to a store."

"Of course not! Only the real thing will do."

"My mother grumbled every Christmas about not having a real Christmas tree. My father mentioned pine needles on the carpet and the time and energy to get rid of the tree, let alone the cost of buying a new one every year, getting the permit…"

"I already have the permit. My dad…" Her voice tapered off. Then, she managed to get it back. "My dad applied for it before he died. It came in the mail a few weeks ago."

"Okay, we'll get a Christmas tree. Isn't December second a little early?"

"I'll keep it watered." Her eyes sparkled, and she looked so beautiful that he leaned down toward her, his lips meeting hers in a gentle kiss that he hoped would go on forever.

The doorbell rang, and Natalie pulled back, seeming dazed. She shrugged out from under his arm, and Lucky grumbled. "I hope it's something important because I'm not crazy about interruptions."

Natalie wasn't crazy about interruptions, either, especially interruptions like Lucky's parents, Mr. and Mrs. Welch, suddenly standing at her front door.

Chapter Twelve

"Where's Robby?" Lucky's mother managed to beat her husband into the room. Lucky came off the couch in a fluid motion that quickly had him standing between his dad and Natalie.

His dad glanced around the living room, the couch Lucky had been sitting on, the Disney movie still playing, silently, on the television and the pictures on the wall. He edged around Lucky, both men looking wary, and walked over to the fireplace. A huge photo of Natalie, her dad and Robby was above it.

"Yes, where's the boy?" Henry Welch demanded.

Natalie felt like she'd lost her breath. "He's sleeping. He went down about an hour ago."

"This is a charming house," Betsy complimented, first shooting a look at her husband. "Perfect for raising a child. If you could pick up our house and move it to the country, it would fit right in."

"Dad, this is not a good time. I was planning to come visit you on Tuesday, talk this over and—"

"And make sure I didn't ruin everything?" Henry raised an eyebrow.

"Well, yes."

"I don't plan to ruin anything."

"Dad, I want— What? What did you say?"

"I don't plan to ruin anything. I accept that Robby is Marcus's son."

Natalie didn't have strength enough to go weak in the knees. Did Mr. Welch know?

Natalie doubted it.

"Lucky, your dad and I had a long talk last night. I told him about your list, the short-term and long-term visitation limits—"

"They're not limits," Natalie said. "They're guidelines."

"Reasonable guidelines," Lucky put in.

"We agree," Betsy said seriously. She looked at her husband. For a moment, Natalie thought she saw fear, but then she saw hope mingled with love, both tinged with doubt. "Your dad and I realized that finding Robby is a gift. We want to get to know him."

Natalie looked at Lucky.

He wasn't buying it, either.

Betsy turned to Natalie. "I won't buy him a pony, I promise. I won't buy a second home here in Selena. But I will make a room for him at our house."

Natalie felt the tears form.

"Please," Betsy said, "may I look at him?"

Natalie led the way, Betsy on her heels. Lucky came third, with Henry slowly taking the rear. They all crowded in the doorway. Betsy only had eyes for Robby. Henry seemed to have eyes for Robby, Natalie and Betsy.

Finally, Natalie saw it. The look a man has for the woman he loves. Henry may be hard to get along with, but he loved his wife.

It gave Natalie a brief moment of hope. She peered into

the bedroom. Robby lay facedown, his feet on the pillow and his head by the baseboard. He snored slightly. A tiny train was clutched in his hand.

"Oh, he's precious," Betsy breathed.

"He's not going to be precious if we wake him up before it's time," Natalie said gently.

Back down the stairs they went. Henry led. He went right back to studying the photos. Betsy did the same, oohing and aahing at every change in Robby.

Lucky went to stand by his father, taking a stance Natalie was starting to recognize. It was the same stance he'd used after jumping off the bull at the Selena rodeo when he'd known he was a winner. It was the same stance he'd taken when he stood in her front yard insisting that he wanted to be included in their lives.

He hadn't needed to use that stance with her lately; the half smile worked just as well.

"So, Dad, why the change of heart, really?"

Natalie saw, then, something Lucky probably missed. Glancing at Betsy, Natalie knew she'd seen it also. Henry aged right in front of their eyes. In the flicker, he'd gone from powerful my-business-is-my-business-and-my-family-is-my-business Henry Welch to an I'm-about-to-lose-everything father.

"Lucky," Natalie said gently.

"No, I want to know. What made you change your mind?"

"Go ahead and tell him," Betsy urged. "You told me. It probably saved our marriage. Maybe you admitting you were wrong will save your relationship with Lucky."

"I was wrong," Henry admitted.

Lucky looked like he was about to say something stupid, something a preacher would never say, like "Big surprise" or maybe "Duh" or even "I don't care."

He didn't say anything. He kept his stance, staring at his father in a way that made him more equal than son.

His dad seemed to recognize the stance as something to be reckoned with. He made a huge effort to regain his power, but the effort didn't reach his eyes. They were sad, so sad.

"I've lost your brother," Henry admitted. "You never come around. Your mother stopped talking to me." He glanced at his wife. "Two solid weeks and not a word, not even a 'Pass me the salt.' Then, on Friday, Bernice sends me an e-mail."

"An e-mail got you here," Lucky said, amazement edging his voice.

"She sent pictures of Robby at her house. She got him eating a piece of chicken, swinging, chasing Mary. They were beautiful. There was one of him on that pretend bull you made over at Bernice's," Lucky's dad said. His voice broke a little. "It was Marcus all over again, at Betsy's dad's place, riding that stupid pretend bull.

"Robby is Marcus's child. I'm a grandparent. I sat all afternoon at my desk, ignoring my secretary, ignoring the phone, ignoring the paperwork gathered in front of me.

"I never harmed you or Marcus," Henry choked. "Not physically, anyway, and for the life of me, I'm not sure why or how I lost you. I've provided—"

"Money," Lucky supplied.

"Yes, a good home, food, the best schooling."

It was father versus son.

"I'd rather have had time, Dad. I'd rather have had your time."

"I… Maybe I—" Henry stuttered.

"Mommy, who dat?" Robby entered the room, rubbing his eyes and staring at Henry.

The room remained silent. Henry didn't look away from Lucky. Betsy was still holding her head in her hands.

"This is Lucky's daddy and mommy," Natalie supplied.

"Oh." Robby looked around the room, finally seeing Betsy. He went right to her, crawled on her lap and settled down.

"Natalie," Lucky suggested, "why don't you and my mother take Robby into the kitchen for a snack or something?"

"Oh, no," Betsy said. "I'm not leaving. There's probably more I need to hear."

"No, Mother, there's not." It was Henry, calling his wife Mother, in that soft voice that denotes love. For all his faults, the man loved his wife. He loved both his sons, too. He just didn't know how to show it.

"Mr. Welch," Natalie said. "Maybe it's best we don't try to change everything today. Why don't you just get to know Robby, and then when both you and Lucky calm down, maybe you can have a conversation that is not heated?"

"My dad—" Lucky began.

"Is here admitting he made some poor choices," Natalie finished.

She waited to see what Lucky would do. Would he turn and march out the door, refusing to even listen? Would he demand that his father leave? Was there hope for forgiveness? Because if Lucky couldn't forgive his father for making poor choices, how would he forgive Natalie for not telling him the truth about Robby's birth?

If Robby hadn't entered the room, Lucky didn't know where the conversation would have gone. Robby simply looked from grown-up to grown-up and finally asked, "What going?"

"Nothing, baby," his mother said. "Just a bit of a family discussion."

"It loud," Robby remarked.

Loud? Lucky thought. The discussion could have been loud, should have been loud, but it was just his father, one more time, proving he didn't see what was right in front of him.

Time was more precious than money.

The only thing different about this confrontation was his father was actually admitting errors.

He studied his dad until he realized he had to make the first move. Again. And he would be the bigger person if he did.

"Natalie's right," he said. "We need to take this slow."

Slow turned out to be the whole family attending the evening church service. Robby didn't make it through the whole service, and for the first time Lucky understood why parents of toddlers seemed to miss evening services. Natalie didn't miss any of the service, though, because Grandma Betsy, with her very willing assistant and best friend, Bernice, was quite happy to sit in the foyer and watch Robby explore every nook and cranny.

Sitting between Natalie and his father, Lucky could only shake his head at the irony. His dad sat all stiff and stern, clearly out of place. Natalie was pale and fidgety, nothing like this morning. Both of them so needed the Word.

What had Natalie been asking about the other night at the café? John 8:32.

"…and the truth will set you free."

Judging by his father's posture, he wasn't feeling free. Judging by Natalie's posture, she wasn't as free as she should be.

After church, his parents headed for their motel after deciding that they would all travel to Delaney the next day to see the church Lucky was considering, and Lucky drove Natalie and Robby home.

He got a kiss from both of them.

Robby's kiss more or less hit his ear. Natalie's landed right where it was supposed to and didn't last nearly long enough.

He wondered, as he drove away, whether he should be kissing a woman whose faith didn't match his, the woman he'd fallen in love with anyway, the woman who should have been his brother's wife! *Oh, God,* Lucky prayed, *you promise us hope and a future, but please, God, let Natalie and Robby be my future.*

Natalie's dad used to moan, "I never get enough sleep," and Natalie had more or less tuned him out. Now she knew what he meant. It was four in the morning, and she was wide-awake. The outside was pitch-black; even the moon was hiding its face. The house was quiet. She padded down the hall and turned on the kitchen light, turned the radio to a country station and dropped a Pop-Tart into the toaster.

Even through her slippers she could feel the coldness of the floor. Winter had stopped knocking on Selena's door. It had arrived.

She went and adjusted the thermostat, then poured a glass of milk, retrieved the Pop-Tart and sat at the kitchen table for a minute. Pure happiness was just out of reach, so close her fingers were skimming the edge of its jacket.

Lucky was wearing the jacket.

She'd allowed herself to get complacent. She'd allowed herself to believe that maybe everything would be all right.

Maybe it would be.

Lucky had not turned on his father. Who knew? Maybe the two of them were out having breakfast right now. Natalie took a bite of her Pop-Tart and signed on to her laptop. This morning, first thing, she had to deal with a hosting issue. Then, she was updating the last of her current clients, and finally she had received signed contracts and initial payment from five new clients. She had lots to do.

None of her tasks took her mind fully off Lucky, his family or her problem. At seven-thirty, she woke Robby up, got him dressed and in front of a bowl of cereal, and went to her bedroom to get herself ready for the day.

When Lucky showed up, he wasn't alone. The trip to Delaney was eye-opening. Betsy was a gem. Not only was she a willing travel guide—she could write a book about the town—but also she took Grandma duty seriously. Robby's coat was quickly zipped, his runny nose wiped and his hand held ever so vigorously. Within hours, she owned the title "Grandma," and Robby said it often.

Grandpa was a different animal. Natalie wasn't one to believe a leopard changed his spots, and in Henry Welch's case, the spots really weren't changing.

Lucky's dad was none too pleased about being a passenger, but Natalie had argued that her car would seat four adults and already held Robby's car seat. Lucky willingly took the front passenger side. Betsy crawled in the center of the backseat and promptly began talking with Robby. Henry sat by the window.

The drive to Delaney wasn't bad, mostly because Henry spent his time talking into his cell phone instead of to his family. Natalie glanced over at Lucky. His lips were thin, and he was staring out the window.

If her dad were in the car, they'd have already stopped for treats and jokes would be rolling off his tongue.

Yeah, she missed her dad.

They arrived at the church about the time Betsy said, "Henry, put away the phone." Except for Robby, it was a pretty solemn group. Robby skipped across the barren parking lot and up the church steps. Lucky was right behind him, key in hand, not quite skipping but moving pretty quickly. A turn of the lock, and they all went in. Natalie liked it on sight. It was clean, small and quaint. A century of memories called out to her. Lucky had mentioned baptisms, funerals and weddings.

"This just might work." Lucky said exactly what she was thinking. Of course, he also said a lot more. "At most, this church holds eighty. I can deal with eighty. What a great opportunity."

The half smile turned to a full smile as he looked around the main auditorium. Natalie followed his scrutiny. She almost smiled, too. He was that excited; it was that contagious. The Delaney church was maybe a third the size of Selena's. The auditorium was a perfect square. Up front was a baptismal and a podium. Two small pews flanked the podium.

Pews took up the lion's share of the auditorium. There were ten on each side. Robby ran between them, his feet sounding too loud in the quiet church.

Suddenly, Natalie realized churches weren't like libraries. Churches were only alive when people crowded their halls.

"Mommy, wook!" Robby held up someone's long-forgotten toy train. He and Betsy promptly sat down and started playing choo-choo.

Henry shook his head. "Eighty doesn't mean eighty putting in the offering. It won't pay rent. It won't pay for insurance. What will you live on?"

"The elders talked to me for a little while last night. If I accept the position, a house comes with the job."

"What kind of a house?" Henry asked.

The house was next to the church. It looked as old as the church, too. One story, two bedrooms and a kitchen the size of Natalie's bedroom closet. A family was renting it. They had three kids and were trying to appear inviting. Clearly, they were terrified at being evicted on account of a preacher.

"I can live in the travel trailer if I decide to stay in

Delaney," Lucky said. "Or I'll go ahead and rent the apartment at Patty's. Her husband talked about hiring me on as a cowpoke if I wanted."

He looked at Natalie. "Of course, you'll need to convince her you approve."

Natalie nodded, swallowing her emotions, and also watching Betsy and Henry. Betsy looked like she wanted to move in with Patty, too. Henry looked like he'd just swallowed the world's biggest lemon.

Before returning to Selena, they drove by Lucky's grandparents' place. Betsy wanted to stop, introduce herself to the people living there, but Henry checked his watch often enough to convince Natalie that this was not the perfect time for a social visit.

"We'll do it next time," she promised Betsy. In essence, she was promising Betsy a next time with Robby. It was okay, because already there had been lots of next times with Lucky.

Natalie reached across the seat and took his hand. She didn't care if his dad saw. She only cared that Lucky knew. She was there for him.

"Drop us off at the motel," Henry instructed. "We need to get back to Austin today. I can only afford to take one day off."

Natalie stole a peek at the rearview mirror. So this Monday counted as a day off for Lucky's dad. He'd spent most of it on his cell phone, the rest spent looking disappointed in his son's choice of a profession, followed by shooting down his wife's desire to visit the home she'd grown up in.

He hadn't really tried to get to know Robby. And, as if sensing it, Robby seemed fascinated by him.

Natalie almost felt sorry for Henry Welch.

There were two motels in Selena, one on each end of the town. The Welches had taken the one closest to the side of town Bernice lived on. Natalie pulled up beside a car with a rental bumper sticker, and Henry had the door open before the car completely came to a stop.

"Mommy, go in?" Robby asked.

"He can come in for a minute?" Betsy asked, following her husband out of the car.

Lucky hopped out, too. "Mom, Natalie needs to get home. She works out of her home and—"

"And I woke up at four this morning and got three hours in, so we can stay a minute." Natalie turned off the ignition. It was Betsy's face that prompted the words, but Henry's face said even more.

Betsy unbuckled Robby, and together Grandma, Grandpa and Robby walked into the motel room. Natalie opened the car door and got out. Lucky followed.

"Your father tried," Natalie said gently. "He's here."

"He tried on his terms."

Inside the motel room, something dropped. Natalie froze. Had Robby knocked something over? Was she about to hear her son wail? Or would she hear Henry Welch's angry voice?

Instead she heard laughter.

Robby came out of the motel room wearing Henry Welch's jacket, a tie, and carrying the man's cell phone.

"I spilled suitcase, Mommy. He picking it up now."

Natalie hurried into the room, intent on helping, but both Betsy and Henry were bent down and chuckling.

"He went for my best tie. I brought three, in case I wound up having to leave Betsy and attend a meeting in Dallas. He didn't want one of my everyday ties, no sirree. He had to have my best."

"The boys never did that," Betsy offered. "They dressed up in my father's clothes."

Some of the leopard's spots faded when Henry managed to say, "Betsy, you want to stay in Selena a few days?"

"I do."

"Then let's pack up your things and get you over to Bernice's."

"Yeah!" Robby said.

"Yeah!" Betsy echoed.

Natalie thought she saw the barest trace of a smile on Henry's face.

Betsy, Robby and Lucky went into the motel room. Natalie didn't move fast enough. She wound up alone with Henry Welch.

As if on cue, Henry's cell phone rang. He reached in his pocket but instead of answering it, he turned it off.

Natalie heard Robby squeal, and she heard Lucky say, "If you're going to jump on the bed, you have to take Grandpa's clothes off it."

She took one step toward the motel door, but Henry's voice stopped her. "Robby's really not yours," Henry said quietly.

She couldn't move. Her legs had turned to cement. She managed to turn, face Lucky's father, and the only words she could manage to squeak were, "How did you know?"

"I've always made it my business to know where my sons were. I know Robby's birthday. I know where Marcus was at that time, and I know you weren't around. Your cousin Tisha was."

Natalie was silent.

Henry looked at her. "Quite frankly, I don't understand. Why would you drop out of college, give up a dream, and all for a boy who really doesn't belong to you?"

"Oh, well, that's the kicker," she said sarcastically. "Tisha pretty much left Robby with me when he was just two weeks old. By the time he was two months and I realized she wasn't coming back, my dad and I stopped looking. He belonged to us."

Natalie nervously studied the motel door. If Lucky came

out now…this would be the worst time…there really would never be a good time.

"They can't hear me," Henry said. "And I don't plan on telling them. It would be just one more heartache after Marcus's death. Betsy has her grandchild, and unless I miss my guess, pretty soon she'll have a daughter-in-law."

To someone else, not someone who'd spent a month going back and forth with a horrible untruth, maybe this would be the answer to the prayer.

Answer to a prayer? Lucky was the answer to her prayer, one she didn't even know she'd been uttering. In front of her, what this man was offering had nothing to do with answering prayers.

Henry Welch was still trying to manipulate his family.

Three years ago Robby had changed her life. Three months ago Lucky had swooped in, done the same thing, and also started changing her heart.

Looking Henry in the eye, she said, "I thank you for not telling Lucky, but I intend to tell him."

Because if she didn't, she was just like Henry Welch.

"I'm not like you," she whispered.

His cheeks reddened, and for the first time, she saw where Lucky got his looks. They were the same. Maybe at one time Henry had even owned a killer half smile. It might explain why Betsy married him.

He shoved his hands in his pockets and turned toward the motel. "Good, because I wouldn't wish being like me on anybody."

Chapter Thirteen

"**W**hat did you say to my dad?" Lucky couldn't believe the change. Not only had Henry agreed to take Betsy to Bernice's, but also he'd decided to stay on an extra day at Bernice's, as well. In all their years, he'd never stayed at Bernice's, preferring a motel, or even preferring to go home while Betsy stayed.

Henry Welch claimed he wanted to get to know Natalie and Robby. Robby didn't seem to mind. Betsy was overjoyed. Lucky was speechless. And Natalie, well, she turned pale, fidgety, and Lucky could tell the main thing on her mind was escape. She and Robby stayed at the motel for a while, but didn't seem inclined to stick around or head to Bernice's.

Tuesday, Natalie dropped Robby off for a whole day with Lucky and his parents. She'd begged off staying, mentioning work and some chores. Lucky, sensing something was amiss, especially since she wouldn't look at him or his father, let her go. He'd get to the bottom of whatever was bothering her—and he sure hoped it wasn't his father—after his parents left.

Yesterday, his parents had taken Robby Christmas shopping and then picked him up again to attend Wednesday night services at the church. They left Thursday morning, and the first thing Lucky did was call Natalie and remind her of their Christmas tree date.

She might have begged off again, but Robby caught enough of the conversation to get excited. In the background, he could hear Robby wanting to see Lucky, wanting to see Grandma, wanting to see Henry.

It wasn't lost on Lucky that Robby referred to Henry Welch as Henry instead of Grandpa. When Natalie told Lucky to hold on and reminded Robby that Grandma and Henry were gone, wails erupted.

So here they were in the middle of a winter wonderland, Robby all smiles, chopping down their own tree. Lucky was having trouble getting Natalie to tell him what was bothering her, and something sure was.

"So, what did you say to my dad?" Lucky repeated. "He not only held my mom's hand yesterday—and I've never seen that—but also he turned his cell phone off for a whole afternoon."

She bit her lip, not something he'd seen her do before, and not something he really wanted to see. It took away from the joy of the day together.

"I guess the real question is, 'What did my dad say to you?' Come on, you can tell me."

The tears spilling from her eyes made him back off. Whatever happened had really upset her.

Anger, pure and hot and white, much more intense than Lucky had felt in years, caused him to step back and let the ax fall to the ground. The snow, as if sensing the intensity of the moment, fell even more heavily.

"What did my dad say?"

She looked at him, and he was reminded of a deer in headlights. He recognized the look from the day at the courthouse.

She'd had the look again on the church steps the first day his mother met Robby. Now, she had it again.

He'd take the blame for the first time only.

"Tell me what my father did."

"Nothing. Your father is not the problem. I am."

She busied herself with helping, making sure she was not looking at him, and also that she was as far away as possible. If he ventured near, she immediately acted as if Robby needed something.

It was a strange dance and not one Lucky was used to. He preferred to deal with things head-on. You draw a bull, you consider the bull's history and you ride the bull. You either win or lose. To Lucky's way of thinking, he'd drawn Natalie; he just needed to get past her connection with his brother. He knew Natalie's history, where she lived, went to school and who she dated, but every time he thought they were a team, something came between them. This time it wasn't a rodeo clown. This time it looked like it was his father.

What he needed was to get Natalie alone on a real date and woo her.

Together, the three of them carted the tree—Robby more a hindrance than a help, but an oh-so-enthusiastic hindrance—to Lucky's truck.

Lucky looked at her. The cold had rosied her cheeks. Her parka only intensified her curves.

This draw was for life. *Please, God, let it be for life.*

"I accepted the church in Delaney," he said. "This time next week, I'll be done with Cowboy Christmas Week. Then I'm also done being a bull rider. I can't imagine anywhere I'd rather be than with my own church, close to you and Robby."

He hoisted the tree in the back of the truck, secured it and then hopped down next to her. "Please tell me what my dad said."

"Nothing I didn't need to hear," Natalie said, walking to the passenger side and helping Robby into the back of the extended cab. It already looked like a dad's truck. The child seat was permanent, toys littered the floor and fish-shaped crackers were smashed into the seat. Natalie brushed some crumbs off Robby's knees before admitting, "Your dad didn't do anything but talk about Robby. Let's drop it. Today is for Robby."

"For me!" Robby echoed.

"No, today is for all of us," Lucky said as he started the engine.

His cell phone rang just as he hit the edge of Selena. His mother's excited voice, too excited for a greeting, immediately jumped into the middle of what she was trying to say "…And there's going to be a Santa Claus, and a Christmas village, and presents for the little ones, and crafts. Your father's the one who saw the sign. We were just driving through Delaney for old time's sake. He said we could stay one more day."

Lucky glanced at Natalie as his mother rambled on. Natalie remained tense.

"I'll call you right back, Mom." He hit the off button and laid the phone in his lap. "Do you know about the Christmas village in Delaney?"

"No," Robby said.

"Yes," Natalie said. "We took Robby last year. He had a great time."

"My parents were driving through Delaney for old time's sake and saw the advertisement. My dad suggested they stay one more day and take Robby."

"Your dad?"

"Yes, I think we're all surprised."

"Another family gathering?"

"Yes!" Robby called from the backseat. Lucky checked the

rearview mirror. The little boy understood way too much. Lucky needed to train himself to watch what he said.

"No," Lucky said. "This would be a grandparents' night out with grandson. Which would leave tonight open for us."

"For us?"

"Yes, a date. A real date. You and me."

She didn't look nearly as excited as he wanted her to look. Usually, when he asked a woman out, she started talking about time, what to wear and what to do.

Natalie just looked at him as if she was terrified.

"Here's what we'll do," he said quickly. "We'll pretend it's a first date."

"What?"

"You can thank Mary for the idea. When we were kids, she'd make Marcus and me play this stupid thing called the 'dating game.' She'd get three chairs. Marcus would sit in one. I'd sit in one. She'd usually put a stuffed animal or a cat in the third. Then, she'd ask us questions before she'd pick who got to date her. Come to think of it—" his words dropped off "—I always got picked."

"I'd have picked you," Natalie said, thawing a little.

Lucky chuckled. "Glad to hear it. Back then, our pretend date was always at a restaurant, and Mary made Marcus be the waiter. I remember being served empty cups of tea and lots of plastic food."

He looked at her, wanting so much and afraid of losing it all. "If we go out tonight, we can pretend it's our first date. We'll act as if we're just getting to know each other because… Well, because you picked me."

Yes, she'd picked him, all right, Natalie thought, staring into her closet. Unfortunately, he believed that she'd picked Marcus first.

Tell him tonight. Tell him you never even met Marcus.

Only that wasn't the most important thing to tell him. She had to tell him that although she was Robby's mother, she hadn't borne him.

She had quite an agenda for a first date.

First things first. Natalie pushed aside some cotton shirts. She'd worn her best outfit that Sunday she'd met them for lunch after service. Everything else added up to Mommy clothes, and there was no time to go shopping.

Great, tonight might be the worst first date of her life and she was worried about what to wear.

She pulled out the outfit she'd worn to church, tossed it on the bed and headed for the shower.

An hour later, she woke Robby from his nap, dressed him warmly, gave him a banana, and together they sat on the swing on the front porch and waited for their dates. A light snow fell. Robby would only make it a minute, but there was something magical about sitting on the swing in a winter wonderland.

Last December, there'd been strings of lights, sparkling reindeer with movable parts and a helium-filled snowman in their front yard.

This year, only the snow signaled Christmas.

"Where going, Mama?" Robby's words came out in white puffs.

"You want to go back inside and wait? Are you cold?"

"I fine. Where going, Mama?"

"You're going to Delaney with Grandma and Henry, remember?"

"Oh, yeah. Mama go, too."

"No, your uncle Lucky and I are going somewhere else."

"I go with you?"

"No, you go with Grandma and Henry."

"I wanna go with you."

Music to her ears. Unfortunately, at that moment, Grandma and Henry arrived. Robby flew from the swing and into his grandmother's arms.

Natalie switched the car seat to their car and gave Robby a big hug as she strapped him in.

"Is there anything he shouldn't eat?" Betsy asked.

"No, he can eat just about anything."

Mundane words, and the type of back-and-forth she could now expect, no, that she prayed she'd be using for years, until Robby grew up and no longer needed Mommy.

Henry got behind the wheel and Robby waved, but still Betsy Welch stood alongside the car, looking at Natalie. Then, as if someone had given her a push, she ran around the car and came at Natalie, crushing her in a tight embrace. "Talk about an answered prayer. Oh, thank you for all this. Thank you."

Natalie felt the tears swell. She swallowed them back and nodded.

He had no idea where to take her.

Usually, on first dates, it was dinner and a movie. But this really wasn't a first date, and this date deserved to be set apart from all others.

The other first dates were with women he might want to get to know. This first date was with a woman he already loved.

Dinner and a movie weren't good enough.

But he absolutely could not come up with any other ideas.

His parents and Robby waved as they drove down the driveway.

Was that a smile on his dad's face?

No, definitely not. Couldn't be, could it? Lucky grinned.

Coming around a curve, he saw Natalie sitting on the porch swing. She had on brown boots, black pants and a sky-blue parka with white edging. Her hair was covered with a matching blue hat.

Imagine coming home every night to this.

He parked and walked toward her, wishing she'd raise her head, look at him and smile.

But she was looking at her hands. He made it all the way to the third step on the porch before she looked up.

"You should be wearing mittens." He took the space next to her and reached for her hands.

She let him.

They were red, cold and felt like heaven.

"What's wrong?"

"Oh, Robby just drove off with your parents, and I'm feeling a little blue."

"It's good for him to be with other people. And you need some adult company. Feel like dinner and a movie?"

She looked at her hands, only this time they were still encased in his. He tightened his grip. No, this was not a first date. First dates didn't feel this good.

"I don't know. I think I've lost my appetite, and I don't know if I'd be focused enough to stay with a movie."

"Okay," he said. "What would you like to do?"

"I don't know."

"Hey, that's the guy's line," he protested.

She smiled, thawing a bit, and took her hands from his and stuck them in her parka pockets.

"So, what is there to do in Selena on a Thursday night?"

She laughed, thawing even more. "Dinner and a movie."

He shifted, stretching his legs out and looking at the land. It was gorgeous. Snow, glistening and perfect, pelted the front yard and stretched across the empty grazing land.

"Last year at this time, what were you doing?"

"Decorating for Christmas."

"Why aren't you doing it this year?"

"With Dad gone…"

Of course, Lucky felt like slapping himself on the fore-head. He'd have done it, too, if he had been with a riding buddy or church friend. He was falling in love with Natalie, but he kept forgetting, or at least he was trying to forget, her past. In his defense, he still had trouble thinking of her with Marcus.

"What kind of decorating did you do?"

"Since Robby turned one, we've had lots of stuff in the yard, a big tree. We used to do a little tree. I have singing Santas and sparkly reindeer with movable parts, and I have a blow-up snowman."

"Well," Lucky said. "I didn't really feel like dinner and a movie, either."

She looked at him. The deer-in-the-headlights look gone.

"Robby would be really impressed if the house was all lit up when my parents dropped him back home."

Her face lit up.

He wished it were more from the idea of decorating with him than the idea of pleasing her son, but he'd take what he could get.

Then, her face fell. "He'll be asleep."

"This would definitely be a good reason to accidentally wake him."

She didn't look convinced.

"I have to leave at eleven tonight, and I'll be gone all weekend. I'd like to say goodbye. Waking him up would mean a lot to me."

"Another rodeo?"

"In Odessa."

"The weather's bad," she argued.

"So…"

Finally, she laughed and affectionately muttered, *"Cowboys."*

The Christmas stuff was stored in the barn where the horses should be. It took him about ten trips to cart the plastic bins—all labeled—either to the front porch or inside the house.

"You do the labeling?" Lucky asked.

"Yeah. Dad had a bad habit of throwing stuff wherever it would fit. Ornaments stayed on the tree, candles melted and when the treetop angel lost her halo, I took over the packing up."

Whatever her father had used to secure the Christmas lights to the rafters was now missing in action. Lucky wound up driving in nails while Natalie handed up oversize paper clips. Thanks to her heavy mittens, she dropped more than she handed. Thanks to cold, bare hands, it took him a lot longer than it should have. Finally, she ran in and got him a pair of her father's gloves. Except for when he also dropped the paper clips, things speeded up. There was some daylight when they finished the porch.

He'd do the roof when he came back.

Because he intended to come back again and again.

By the time the movable reindeer were nodding their heads, it was almost dark. Fifteen minutes later, the inflatable snowman became a glowing beacon in blackness.

It was time to move inside.

Natalie had already positioned the tree in a stand close to the front window. She had it in water. Lucky checked to see if it was near a heat register. It wasn't.

"Robby should be here for this." Natalie opened a box of ornaments.

Outside, they'd been moving, laughing and tossing an occasional snowball at each other.

Inside, their fingers ached from the cold, and if Lucky guessed correctly, Natalie was suddenly remembering other Christmases—Christmases that involved Robby, her father— and Robby's father? He shook the thought away.

"Do you want to stop?"

She didn't answer.

"I am hungry." He gave her an out.

"Oh!" She looked up, chagrined. "You're right. We needed to eat hours ago." She closed the box of ornaments.

Lucky felt oddly disappointed. He hadn't decorated a tree in years. His mother still did, but if he made it home for Christmas it was just that one day. He really no longer even noticed the tree.

He noticed this one because he noticed the woman it belonged to.

She moved to the kitchen, and he watched her walk. No limp. No stress?

"How about grilled cheese and tomato soup?" she called.

He looked out the window, the one somewhat blocked by a tree waiting for decorations. Snow was starting to fall; the Christmas lights blinked away the darkness. On the wall next to the tree was a photo of Natalie and Robby.

"Perfect."

He wasn't talking about the meal choice.

"Good, give me a minute," she called.

He had no intention of sitting alone in the living room. He moved to the kitchen and watched her.

"Want me to set the table?" he asked.

She looked at him. A few strands of hair fell in her eyes, and she blew them away. "Sure."

It was a nice meal. Just Lucky and Natalie, sitting at the

kitchen table, staring out the window at a tiny winter wonderland they'd created. Then they'd stare at each other. Each
time Lucky tried to turn the look into something more than
innocent appraisal, she looked away.

"Robby should be home any minute," she said.

She was telling him to wait.

Why? He wanted to know why!

"Did you see that?" He pointed out the window. "A
shooting star."

"You can't see shooting stars during a snowstorm," she
said pragmatically.

"Who says?"

She didn't have an answer.

"When I was little," Lucky said, "Mom and I used to make
wishes on shooting stars."

"Yeah, so did I."

"If you could make a wish, right now, what would it be?"

"I'd wish that there were no secrets between us. That this
custody battle was over. And that we were still doing things like
visiting churches, eating at the diner and decorating for Christmas." Her answer was so quick, so honest, that it surprised him.

"Natalie, that wish can come true."

She shook her head.

"Natalie, we need to talk."

She put down her spoon and frowned. "You said this was
a first date. We are talking. Probably too much."

He raised his hands innocently, halting the conversation.
He was halfway relieved because had the conversation continued, he'd have had to share his wish.

I wish that I'd met you first before my brother did.

"Okay, okay. So, the rodeo tomorrow in Odessa. Why
don't you and Robby come?"

"I don't do rodeos."

"You met me at a rodeo."

She wrinkled her nose. "Yes, but I had an ulterior motive for being there."

"If you come to the rodeo tomorrow, I'll be glad to give you another ulterior motive for being there."

"Like what?"

"Like I'll take you and Robby out for steaks afterward."

She shrugged. "You gotta try harder than that."

He leaned forward, reaching across the table for the hand she had loosely wrapped around a glass of milk. He entwined his fingers with hers. "I'd really like you to come. Just once, I want my girl in the audience. I've never really had anyone other than fans or my mother cheer me on. It will be something we can tell our children."

"Our children!"

"Don't sound so surprised."

"Lucky, we're pretending this is a first date! We haven't known each other long enough for commitment."

"How long did you know my brother?"

She jerked her hand out of his.

He sat back, studying her. Why was she so skittish? Why didn't she want to talk about his brother? Maybe, if they could work through Marcus, they could both heal—together.

Lucky started to say something, thought better of it and concentrated on eating. He finished the last of his soup and pushed the plate away. The grilled cheese was long gone.

So was his heart.

He didn't want this to be a first date. He wanted it to be a last date. Truthfully, he wanted to be setting a date. But it was much too soon and there was baggage between them. Baggage she didn't want to talk about yet.

"I'm leaving soon. I need to get to Odessa and settle in. The event starts at five. You'll have fun."

"What if you get hurt?"

"I could have slipped off the ladder when you kept throwing paper clips at me."

"You know what I mean. Bulls are even more dangerous than horses. One wrong turn and—"

"Won't happen. I promise."

"You can't promise."

"It didn't happen last time you watched me ride."

"Last time I watched you ride I didn't…"

"Didn't what?" Lucky urged. "Didn't love me?"

"I don't love you, but Robby does." She looked out the window. "I sure hope this eases up before tomorrow. I don't want you driving all the way to Odessa in bad weather."

He smiled. It was all he needed. She worried about him.

The phone rang, loud against the silence of their once again locked stares.

She started. Good, she was just as befuddled as he was.

He could hear her in the living room and decided to impress her with his domesticatedness. He cleared the table, rinsed the dishes and wiped up all the crumbs. He got to the living room in time to hear her say, "So, she'll sign the guardianship papers?"

If that didn't peak his interest, then the sentence she uttered next did. "What do you mean she's going to have another baby?"

Definitely a private conversation. He started to head back to the kitchen, but paused.

Why would Natalie need guardianship papers?

He stayed, not wanting to eavesdrop, wishing she'd turn and see him and hoping she was talking to Patty about a mutual friend.

She did finally turn. Gone was the deer in the headlights; here was the stunned deer staring down the barrel of the gun.

"Tell Tisha that I'll do my best not to let her current boy-friend find out about Robby."

"Find out what about Robby?" Lucky asked.

"Goodbye." Natalie hung up the phone.

Silence, falling heavily like the snow outside, enveloped the room.

He'd learned from his mother—who had to deal every day with his father—to ask easy questions. "Who was on the phone?"

"The private detective my father hired."

"What did he have to say?"

She didn't answer.

"Did he find out what happened to your father's money?"

"He happened to my father's money," Natalie said.

"What? Oh."

In the distance, the sound of a car rose above the wind of the storm. Lights flashed briefly in the window. His parents were in the front drive. A door opened; a door slammed. Robby squealed.

Natalie said softly, "Ever since your brother died, my father's been trying to find Tisha. He was afraid Tisha might come hunting for Robby. He was afraid your family would find out about Robby. He was afraid you'd want Robby."

"What does Tisha have to do with this, with Robby?"

She cried silently, tears streaming down her face and not a single sob. Her breaths came out in jerks, and he could see her chest heaving. He thought about going to her, but his feet wouldn't move.

They wouldn't move.

"I didn't know your brother," she said. "I never met him."

Lucky felt stupid, slow. This wasn't something he could fix with a hammer, nail and paper clip. This wasn't something an eight-second ride would wipe away. This wasn't something the Good Book had an immediate answer to. At least not one he could think of right away.

"You mean, Marcus isn't Robby's father?"

"No." Natalie shook her head. "No, I mean *I* didn't give birth to Robby. Tisha did."

Chapter Fourteen

"Mommy! Dere's lights. Everywhere!" Robby burst through the door.

Natalie tore her gaze from Lucky's. Five more minutes. That was all she'd needed. Maybe then Lucky would have stormed out of the room, letting her know all her worries were justified and had just tripled. Or maybe he'd have listened to her, listened to how afraid she was, how much she wanted to tell him the truth, but how vulnerable she felt.

Instead, she saw him wince when Robby said *Mommy*.

Surely, the bull rider some called "The Preacher" knew sometimes the best mommies were not the only ones who gained weight for nine months, not the ones who went through labor, not the ones who…

Oh, who was she kidding?

There were no words to tell the man, his family, either, just how much Robby meant to her and her dad.

"Mommy here," Natalie said, looking at Lucky when she said it.

He nodded, but it didn't really look like a yes. He took his coat from the hook by the door, looked at her and no one else and then he walked out.

"You told him," Henry Welch accused.

"Mommy, come look at lights!" Robby raced for her hand, tugged at it. "Pease."

It was impossible to say no to Robby. He practically jumped up and down. Not only was he excited about the lights, but also it was hours after his bedtime. He had antlers on his head, bits and pieces of broken candy cane in his hair and chocolate smears on his shirt.

"Mommy," he reminded. "Lights."

She didn't stop for her coat. Nothing would chase the chills away tonight. The cold slapped her in the face and she started to hurry after Lucky, but Robby was looking up at the lights. "You do dis?"

"Lucky and I did it."

"Unca Lucky!" Robby called.

Lucky paused at the truck door.

Robby carefully went down the front steps and then raced toward the driveway.

"What's going on?" Betsy said.

Neither Natalie nor Henry answered. Lucky bent down and said something to Robby, gave the boy a hug and then hopped in the truck and drove away.

"Henry, are you going to tell me—"

"I will tell you, Betsy," Henry said. "Natalie, we're going to Odessa tomorrow for Lucky's rodeo. Did he already invite you?"

"Rodeo!" Robby whooped as he ran toward them. He stopped in the yard and kicked the oversize, glowing snowman.

"Robby!" both Natalie and Betsy scolded.

"He did invite me," Natalie said once Robby switched his attention to the reindeer, "but that was before I told him about Tisha."

Betsy Welch dropped her purse. She didn't bend to pick it up.

"We're leaving at about three," Henry repeated. "Let's just leave the car seat in the Cadillac."

"No, I'm not going."

"Henry, what's going on?" Betsy Welch didn't sound happy. Natalie didn't blame her. Tisha had that effect on people. After Henry told Betsy the truth about Robby's parentage, Natalie would have that effect on Betsy.

And Lucky.

Robby stomped up the porch stairs, studied the overhead lights again and said "Wow" one more time.

"Mommy," he started. He didn't continue. He stopped to rub his eyes, apparently got snow in them and started to cry. He immediately raised his hands to Natalie. "Up."

"We're coming by at three," Henry said.

"I—" Natalie bent and picked Robby up. He gave her a wet kiss and then turned so he could watch Henry and Betsy.

"I'm not bossing you. I'm giving you an opportunity. You're a strong woman—" Henry looked around, his perusal ending when his eyes met his wife's "—like my Betsy. You're raising a son, you're keeping a home, and for the last few months you've managed to not only make my youngest son fall in love with you, but also enraptured his mother."

"Oh, Henry, hush," Betsy said.

"On top of that, Bernice approves of you." He chuckled. "She sure doesn't approve of me."

Neither Betsy nor Natalie said anything.

"If you decide to attend the rodeo tomorrow, we'll be glad to drive you."

"Rodeo, Mommy, I wanna go rodeo."

"Of course you do."

Natalie did, too.

* * *

It was a good day to come in last place. Lucky'd gotten no sleep, and if you looked up *foul mood* in the dictionary…his picture was on the page. Half of him wanted to jump for joy. Natalie hadn't been with his brother. The other half wanted to punch holes in a wall. Why hadn't she told him? Well, he knew why, really, but the knowledge didn't make the truth any easier to stomach. The last two months had been based on a lie. And because he was naive, he'd bought into the whole facade.

Next to him a foul-mouthed contestant cussed his draw. "Stupid bull. He's rank, and I drew him. Not what I need right now. Not what I need."

Lucky managed to look sympathetic. He wasn't thrilled with his draw, either. He'd wanted the big orange-and-brown-striped bull. In Steamboat Springs, the cowboy on the orange and brown took first place. But there were worse things than WannaBee, the bull Lucky had drawn, and Lucky had as much chance of doing eight seconds on a known bucker as he did a spinner or jumper. Of course, today, what he really needed, to make sure he at least made a second, was to draw a bull named Whimper.

"You keep looking at the stands. You finally got a girl?"

Lucky scowled.

"That explains why you're not doing so hot," the cowboy said.

He scanned the crowd one more time. It was stupid, really. No way was she coming to the rodeo. No way did he want her to come. He'd left her with his parents. According to his cell phone, his mother had called ten times and his dad twice. Twice meant his dad was serious. She'd told them something, and he wasn't ready to find out what.

Natalie hadn't called.

And he hadn't called her.

He had found a scripture, but it did more to soften his heart than harden it.

He thought of Proverbs 3, *"Never walk away from someone who deserves help; your hand is God's hand for that person."*

He'd gotten Natalie to church.

And she wasn't much of a liar. The whole time he knew she was keeping something and it was eating at her.

He'd invited her; he'd left her standing on the porch; it was over. She wasn't there.

He headed for the metal chute. WannaBee? Stupid name for a bull. The name should be WannaYouOffaMyBack.

"Want some help?" the other cowboy said. Lucky finally recognized him. Billy Sam, out of Albuquerque. Not a bad sort, really.

"Yeah, that'd be great."

Billy wrapped the rope around Lucky's wrist, leaving room for it to slip, just slightly, upon the animal's departure. Lucky wondered if time was going as slow as it felt. He walked toward the bucking chute. The smell of sweat, both human and bull, permeated the air. Even though time was standing still, Lucky managed to make his way to WannaBee's back. His legs dropped to WannaBee's side, and he slid toward the rope holding him to the bull. His other hand was in the air.

Yet again, since Marcus died, Lucky was doing the circuit alone. It had never bothered him as much as it did today.

Lucky wanted Natalie, and Robby, to see this, see him ride, see him win! *See that he wouldn't fall.*

"Go!"

The man at the gate flipped the handle, loudly, and the gate flew open. WannaBee snorted in anger. Power, speed and air rushed across Lucky's face. Whoa, everything happened so fast. The bull was fast, maybe faster than Lucky. He turned, bucked and ducked his head toward the ground. He spun left,

again and again and again. WannaYouOffaMyBack, yup,
that's what his name should have been. WannaBee knew the
game, but so did Lucky. A buzzer sounded. Lucky reached
for the tail of the rope, pulling it to untie the tangled hand that
kept him secure on the back of the bull, and with one last burst
of energy—Lucky couldn't say where it came from—he
hurtled off WannaBee, landed on the ground, thought about
his broken toes and tumbled. WannaBee, spent, ran off.

The crowd cheered.

Eight seconds.

And in the crowd, standing up, clapping, was Natalie.

She'd been enjoying for the first time in years the true
meaning of rodeo, of rooting for someone, and thinking
maybe she could get on a horse, maybe, maybe, maybe, when
she'd felt a shift next to her.

"Dat was Unca Lucky?" Robby asked.

"That was Unca Lucky," Natalie responded. The man
who'd held on to a steaming locomotive and jumped off its
back was Lucky. Their Lucky.

"He okay?"

Betsy pulled Robby onto her lap and buried her chin in the
top of his hair. "He's okay." She looked at Natalie and then
bowed her head. "Everything is going to be okay."

Her lips were moving; Natalie knew a prayer when she saw
it. What a surprise. According to Henry, Betsy had barely
flinched when Henry told her the truth about Robby's birth.
She'd called Natalie five times since breakfast, and each and
every time thanked Natalie for being Robby's mommy.

God is with me.

Natalie squirmed. Where did that thought come from? It
was definitely more a Lucky thought than a Natalie thought,
and it was straight from the Bible he'd lent her.

The message was as straightforward as the man who'd lent her the Bible.

"God is with me," Natalie whispered.

He'd been with her as she worked this morning, as she cared for Robby, as she made lunch, and as she dressed them both for a rodeo she had no intention of attending.

Lucky, fresh from a winning ride and full of raw power, came and sat beside her, so close she could feel the heat from his body. "I didn't fall."

The fans who were following him stopped. No one asked for an autograph. They seemed to sense this was a private moment. They faded from sight.

"No, you didn't fall."

"And if I had, I'd have picked myself up, bleeding, broken, and I'd have made my way over to sit by you."

"Betsy," Henry said, "this might be a good time to take Robby for a potty break."

"Even after last night?" Natalie whispered.

"Especially after last night."

"I made up my mind to tell you the truth weeks ago, but the right moment…there never was a right moment."

"Natalie," Lucky interrupted, "I didn't fall *in* the arena, but I did fall outside of it. I fell for you."

"I love Robby," Natalie whispered.

"Well, good," he said, almost chuckling.

How could he chuckle at a time like this?

"I'm not his biological mother," she said. "Ever since the day I approached you at the rodeo, I've been so afraid. I probably have no claim on Robby, not compared to you."

"You've got quite a claim," Lucky said gently. "You've got a whole town full of people who've watched you mother him."

"But—"

"Natalie, you've been worried this whole time that I could take Robby away from you. I understand that. Oh, it shocked me last night. I cannot tell you how I wish I'd known the burden you carried. We wasted a lot of time dancing around the wrong issues."

Natalie patted her leg. "I can't dance."

"Well, darling, you're going to have to learn because I don't want to take Robby away from you. As a matter of fact, I want to stand beside you, raise him as my own. Just think of what we can do *together*."

God is really with me, Natalie thought. Then, humanity knocked. Natalie felt her hands drop to her sides; she felt weak and scared. Stupid tears, they spilled over as she looked up at Lucky. "I don't deserve this."

"You're right," Lucky agreed. "You deserve so much more. But I'm hoping I'll do. With God, all things are possible. I'm the luckiest man I know. Don't you know?" He pulled her into his arms. "How can you not know…? All this time I was worried about what really went on between you and Marcus. As much as I loved my brother…" Lucky choked up. "I was sitting in my truck last night, in the dark, looking at the sky where we saw the shooting star, and I was thinking about my wish. I wished that I'd met you first. I had my Bible open, and I was searching for a scripture on how to deal with you not being Robby's mother, with you not telling me the truth. Finally, I realized I didn't need a scripture to tell me God had answered my prayer."

Natalie buried her head in the crook of his neck for a moment and then looked up at him, knowing she never wanted to look away. It was there, close enough she could touch it. This man was offering her the chance for a family. She saw it in his eyes, she felt it in his touch, and right there in front of a stadium of rodeo fans, right now, she cherished it in his kiss.

His fingers finally slipped away from her cheeks, and his lips left the warmth of hers. She immediately wanted them back.

"You know," she said carefully, "it's really not that far from my place to Delaney. Maybe the first thing we should have in that new church of yours is a wedding."

"Ours?" Lucky said hopefully.

"Ours," Natalie agreed.

* * * * *

Dear Reader,

What fun to write a story with not only a faith element, but also with a rodeo, roots and romance. Natalie and Lucky, the heroine and hero in *Daddy for Keeps,* are special characters who had to overcome self-doubt, the judgment of others and secrets.

Natalie, whom I thought of as a mother bear, quickly became someone who spoke to me. First, she was dealing with an issue that is near and dear to my heart: raising a child. She happened to be raising a child she didn't give birth to, and for most of the story she dealt with the fear of perhaps losing the child, who, by every thought, memory and deed was hers. My parents dealt with the same issue. I am an adopted child, and an adopted *only* child, and my parents, by every thought, memory and deed, let me know that adoption was just a word and that the words *Mommy* and *Daddy* were more than just words.

Then there was Lucky, a rugged hero who managed to be a diamond in the rough. He's a man of faith and character. I know many Luckys, and in real life, I even managed to marry one!

Thank you for reading *Daddy for Keeps.* I love hearing from my readers. Please visit my blog, http://ladiesofsuspense.blogspot.com, or my Web site, www.pamelakayetracy.com. You may also contact me c/o Steeple Hill Books, 233 Broadway, Suite 100l, New York, New York 10279.

Pamela Tracy

QUESTIONS FOR DISCUSSION

1. At the beginning of the novel, Natalie is worried about money. She has to make decisions that affect not only the way she's raising Robby, but also *where* she raises Robby. What is the catalyst that sends her to Lucky? Would you have made such a choice?

2. From the beginning, Lucky is very careful in how he deals with his parents. Does he make the right choice in waiting to tell them about Robby?

3. Lucky's brother caused a lot of grief. We know some of the things Lucky did to try to "save" Marcus. None of them worked. What scripture could help Lucky deal with the loss of his brother? Could the same scripture help his mother? His father? Or, what scripture might they need to turn to?

4. Natalie simply lets people believe Robby belongs to her. Why? Is this what you would do? Name some benefits to this approach. Name some negatives to this approach.

5. When Natalie first has to "share" Robby, what is her biggest fear? How does she deal with it? What is your biggest fear? How do you deal with it?

6. During Natalie's visit to Wednesday-night services, she hears about birth order. She thinks about being an only child, and Lucky talks about his position. Are you an only? A oldest? A middle? A youngest? How has your placement in the family affected your life?

7. What are Lucky's mother's strongest points? Weakest points? Is there a spiritual change she needs to make? What are Lucky's father's strongest points? Weakest points? What change does he make by the end of the story? Will it last?

8. When does Lucky start to fall in love with Natalie? What is it he likes best about her? When does Natalie start to fall in love with Lucky? What is it she likes best about him? Think of someone you love. What do you like best about them? Now, tell them.

9. Is there any hope for Tisha's redemption? What do you think shaped her? What will it take to change her? If she finds the Lord and repents, what should be her role in Robby's life?

10. Lucky decides to leave the rodeo and take a congregation. What are some of the obstacles he will face? Natalie will go from being unchurched to being a preacher's wife. What advice would you give her?

Love Inspired
HISTORICAL

*Powerful, engaging stories of romance, adventure
and faith set in the past—when things were simpler
and faith played a major role in everyday lives.*

Turn the page for a sneak preview of
THE MAVERICK PREACHER
by
Victoria Bylin

*Love Inspired Historical—love and faith
throughout the ages*

M r. Blue looked into her eyes with silent understanding and she wondered if he, too, had struggled with God's ways. The slash of his brow looked tight with worry, and his whiskers were too stubbly to be permanent. Adie thought about his shaving tools and wondered when he'd used them last. Her new boarder would clean up well on the outside, but his heart remained a mystery. She needed to keep it that way. The less she knew about him, the better.

"Good night," she said. "Bessie will check on you in the morning."

"Before you go, I've been wondering…"

"About what?"

"The baby… Who's the mother?"

Adie raised her chin. "I am."

Earlier he'd called her "Miss Clarke" and she hadn't corrected him. The flash in his eyes told her that he'd assumed she'd given birth out of wedlock. Adie resented being judged, but she counted it as the price of protecting Stephen. If Mr. Blue chose to condemn her, so be it. She'd done nothing for which to be ashamed. With their gazes locked, she waited for the criticism that didn't come.

Instead he laced his fingers on top of the Bible. "Children are a gift, all of them."

"I think so, too."

He lightened his tone. "A boy or a girl?"

"A boy."

The man smiled. "He sure can cry. How old is he?"

Adie didn't like the questions at all, but she took pride in her son. "He's three months old." She didn't mention that he'd been born six weeks early. "I hope the crying doesn't disturb you."

"I don't care if it does."

He sounded defiant. She didn't understand. "Most men would be annoyed."

"The crying's better than silence…. I know."

Adie didn't want to care about this man, but her heart fluttered against her ribs. What did Joshua Blue know of babies and silence? Had he lost a wife? A child of his own? She wanted to express sympathy but couldn't. If she pried into his life, he'd pry into hers. He'd ask questions and she'd have to hide the truth. *Stephen was born too soon and his mother died. He barely survived. I welcome his cries, every one of them. They mean he's alive.*

With a lump in her throat, she turned to leave. "Good night, Mr. Blue."

"Good night."

A thought struck her and she turned back to his room. "I suppose I should call you Reverend."

He grimaced. "I'd prefer Josh."

* * * * *

*Don't miss this deeply moving
Love Inspired Historical story
about a man of God who's lost his way
and the woman who helps him rediscover
his faith—and his heart.
THE MAVERICK PREACHER
by Victoria Bylin
available February 2009.*

*And also look for
THE MARSHAL TAKES A BRIDE
by Renee Ryan,
in which a lawman meets his match
in a feisty schoolteacher with
marriage on her mind.*

Love Inspired
HISTORICAL
INSPIRATIONAL HISTORICAL ROMANCE

Adelaide Clark has worked hard to raise her young son on her own, and Boston minister Joshua Blue isn't going to break up her home. As she grows to trust Joshua, Adie sees he's only come to make amends for his past. Yet Joshua's love sparks a hope for the future that Adie thought was long dead—a future with a husband by her side.

Look for

The Maverick Preacher
by
VICTORIA BYLIN

Available February 2009
wherever books are sold.

Steeple Hill®

www.SteepleHill.com

REQUEST YOUR FREE BOOKS!

2 FREE INSPIRATIONAL NOVELS
PLUS 2
FREE
MYSTERY GIFTS

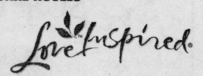

YES! Please send me 2 FREE Love Inspired® novels and my 2 FREE mystery gifts (gifts are worth about $10). After receiving them, if I don't wish to receive any more books, I can return the shipping statement marked "cancel". If I don't cancel, I will receive 4 brand-new novels every month and be billed just $4.24 per book in the U.S. or $4.74 per book in Canada, plus 25¢ shipping and handling per book and applicable taxes, if any*. That's a savings of over 20% off the cover price! I understand that accepting the 2 free books and gifts places me under no obligation to buy anything. I can always return a shipment and cancel at any time. Even if I never buy another book, the two free books and gifts are mine to keep forever.

113 IDN ERXA   313 IDN ERWX

Name	(PLEASE PRINT)	
Address		Apt. #
City	State/Prov.	Zip/Postal Code

Signature (if under 18, a parent or guardian must sign)

Order online at www.LoveInspiredBooks.com

Or mail to Steeple Hill Reader Service:

IN U.S.A.: P.O. Box 1867, Buffalo, NY 14240-1867
IN CANADA: P.O. Box 609, Fort Erie, Ontario L2A 5X3

Not valid to current subscribers of Love Inspired books.

Want to try two free books from another series?
Call 1-800-873-8635 or visit www.morefreebooks.com

* Terms and prices subject to change without notice. N.Y. residents add applicable sales tax. Canadian residents will be charged applicable provincial taxes and GST. Offer not valid in Quebec. This offer is limited to one order per household. All orders subject to approval. Credit or debit balances in a customer's account(s) may be offset by any other outstanding balance owed by or to the customer. Please allow 4 to 6 weeks for delivery. Offer available while quantities last.

Your Privacy: Steeple Hill Books is committed to protecting your privacy. Our Privacy Policy is available online at www.SteepleHill.com or upon request from the Reader Service. From time to time we make our lists of customers available to reputable third parties who may have a product or service of interest to you. If you would prefer we not share your name and address, please check here. ☐

LIREG08R

TITLES AVAILABLE NEXT MONTH

Don't miss these four stories on sale
January 27, 2009.

APPRENTICE FATHER by Irene Hannon
With an orphaned niece and nephew depending on him,
commitment-shy Clay Adams calls upon nanny Cate Shepard
to save them all. With God's help and her kind, nurturing ways,
Cate may be able to ease the children into their new life. And her
love could give lone-wolf Clay the forever family he deserves.

THEIR SMALL-TOWN LOVE by Arlene James
Eden, OK

A high school reunion means a trip home for new Christian
Ivy Villard…to mend some fences. Past mistakes await her
in tiny Eden, Oklahoma—like her former high school sweetheart,
Ryan Jeffords. Yet a second chance at love is waiting for them,
if they're brave enough to take it.

A COWBOY'S HEART by Brenda Minton
A lot of folks depend on ex-rodeo star Clint Cameron, including
his twin four-year-old nephews. So why can't his stubborn
neighbor, Willow Michaels, accept a little help with her
bull-raising business? Clint's got a lot more than advice to offer
Willow, if only she'd look deep in his faithful, loving heart.

BLUEGRASS COURTSHIP by Allie Pleiter
Kentucky Corners

Rebuilding the church's storm-damaged preschool is easy for
the celebrity host of TV's *Missionnovation*, Drew Downing.
Rebuilding lovely hardware store owner Janet Bishop's faith in
God and love may be a bit more challenging. But Drew is just the
man for the job.

LICNMBPA0109